SHEEP
HERDERS
WOLVES

WHY WE ARE WHERE WE ARE
A MODERN AMERICAN FABLE

Scott F. Paradis

https://ScottFParadis.com

Books by **Scott F. Paradis:**

Sheep, Herders, Wolves
Why We Are Where We Are: A Modern American Fable

EXPLOSIVE LEADERSHIP
The Ultimate Leader Training Experience

MONEY
The New Science of Making It

High Performance Health and Fitness Habits
Engage Your Health and Fitness Auto-Pilot

High Performance Habits
Making Success a Habit

How to Succeed at Anything
In 3 Simple Steps

Success 101 How Life Works
Know the Rules, Play to Win

Warriors Diplomats Heroes
Why America's Army Succeeds
Lessons for Business and Life

Promise and Potential
A Life of Wisdom, Courage, Strength, and Will

And coming soon:

Build Me a Son
Hope and Courage Forge a Man

Be
A Messenger of Hope,
An Example of Faith and an Expression of Love

Are You Really Better Than Average?
Where You Stand and the Fastest Way to the Top

Life changing online courses and workshops by
Scott F. Paradis:

Explosive Leadership
The Ultimate Leader Training Experience

MONEY
The New Science of Making It

High Performance Health and Fitness HABITS
Engage Your Health and Fitness Auto-Pilot

Success 101 How Life Works
Focus on Fundamentals

Looking for a motivating presenter?

Scott F. Paradis
Keynote Themes:

SHEEP HERDERS WOLVES
The Time for You to Lead is NOW

MONEY, MONEY, MONEY
An Uncomfortable Truth

Nothing Out of the Ordinary
Everything's Extraordinary
It's as Great as You THINK

SHEEP, HERDERS, WOLVES
Why We Are Where We Are: A Modern American Fable

Published and distributed by:

Cornerstone Achievements
New Hampshire, Virginia, Alaska USA
www.cornerstone-achievements.com

ISBN: 978-0-9863821-7-8 (print, soft cover)
ISBN: 978-0-9863821-6-1 (digital)

Published in the United States of America.

This book is dedicated to
Arthur C. Paradis
We miss you Dad.

And to all the men and women who willingly
take on the mantle of leadership.
The world desperately needs the example of
principled, selfless leaders.

CONTENTS

SHEEP, HERDERS, WOLVES
WHY WE ARE WHERE WE ARE
A MODERN AMERICAN FABLE

- 1 -

THE MANY SERVE THE FEW

Jeff couldn't believe his luck – the questions on his final exam were nearly a duplicate set of the problems he and his study team had been practicing all week. Jeff's professor had explained she was not likely to surprise them on their final final of the term, but an ambitious, energetic, somewhat skeptical university student could never be sure.

Jeff was able to knock out the comprehensive financial mathematics exam in a few minutes under three hours. When he laid down his pencil for the last time and pressed "submit," forwarding his exam for scoring, Jeff felt conflicted. While he had inched one step closer to completing his college journey, he felt angst in anticipation of what was appearing on the horizon: winter break and then his final semester of college. Real life, with all its challenges and opportunities was fast approaching.

One more term, and a four-year university education would come to a close. It was the culmination of a dream Jeff's grandfather expressed when he held Jeff for the very

1

first time. He exclaimed, quite adamantly, his grandson would be the first in his family to go to college.

As if the sun were rising, Jeff could see the hazy glow brightening, bringing pale color to shades of grey as the early rays radiated over the distant skyline, fanning out in every direction. Promise and potential were in the offing. Jeff couldn't stop the sun from rising; rather, he was eagerly anticipating a new dawn. With anxiety and excitement he was ready to embrace the daylight and revel in whatever the sunshine might bring.

As he had been advised, Jeff pursued a STEM (science, technology, engineering and math) course of study, majoring in biology with a minor in economics. His financial mathematics course was the last requirement for his economics minor. He found that he enjoyed economics so much that he had signed up for an elective in global markets in his final term – icing on the cake. His senior biology seminar, part two, in the spring semester would nail down his biology major. Everything was falling into place.

So, what next?

Jeff possessed an inherent curiosity about how life worked. He enjoyed sports, he enjoyed academics, and he even enjoyed working – making a contribution, earning money while helping people get what they want. At the age of eight, he had begun helping with the family business, a popular bakery and café in his hometown. His parents, his aunt, and unequivocally his grandfather, told him, "In this family, every member contributes." And contribute Jeff did.

Drawing near the end of his college journey, Jeff was preparing himself to move to the next phase of life. He wanted to explore the world and he was keen to test himself both intellectually and physically. As far as he was concerned, no challenge was too big and no problem too intractable. He just had to gain the right perspective, join together with the right team, and then apply the right energy. Youthful optimism was Jeff's defining quality, and that optimism, tempered with a realistic dose of cynicism, were common characteristics of his circle of friends.

Now that his exams were over, he had a few hours of free time before he had to be at the bar and grill for his last shift before winter break. Tomorrow he would make the two-hour drive home, perhaps for the last lengthy stay in his childhood bedroom. Maybe he could squeeze in a little Fortnite with José before reporting to work.

José was likely already online; when he wasn't in class or studying, José was adventuring in cyberspace. Fortnite was José's latest passion. Jeff knew José had finished his last final that morning. Perhaps José and some other gamers would be up for Fortnite exploits in creative mode.

The foray into Fortnite was an adventure, as always, but duty called. The office beckoned. Jeff's office wasn't exactly an "office," though. He worked at The Thirsty Scholar, a college-town dive bar just to the north of The Ohio State University campus. Jeff had already spent a lifetime, albeit a brief lifetime, in food service, and since he was warned against taking on debt from an early age, he always worked and saved. Jeff was going to complete his bachelor's degree and have some money in the bank as he launched his career.

Having worked at his family's bakery and café since he was a kid, he was comfortable serving in any and every position in a food service establishment. He had started at the café washing dishes and cleaning up in the kitchen. Then he moved up to bussing tables. After a few years of grunt work he began to assist with baking duties. On non-school days, he was up at four o'clock in the morning. Pastries and coffee were staples in his blue-collar hometown of Lorain, Ohio. Eventually he graduated to counter work, and finally culinary duties in the kitchen. By the time he had completed high school, he could easily manage the entire operation, and served as welcome relief for his mother and aunt, who were now the primary operators of what had been his grandfather's business.

While working his way through college, Jeff decided to stick with what he knew – food service – using the opportunity to expand his culinary repertoire. He didn't exactly need the money to complete his degree; he had more than enough set aside, as his grandfather, affectionately known as Papa, had set Jeff down at the age of eight and proposed a deal.

Jeff – referred to as Jefferson by Papa as he was named after Thomas Jefferson, the American patriot and third president of the United States whom Papa had always admired – would be the first in the family to go to college, but he had to earn his way through. He would have to do well in school and he would have to save. As Jeff had been contributing at the café, Papa offered him permanent work, and a deal: for every dollar Jeff saved for college, Papa would match it. Over the course of ten years, with Papa managing his investments, Jeff was able to accumulate a college fund of nearly eighty thousand dollars – more than enough to get through a good state school.

Not liking to see an account balance decline, Jeff continued to work while attending college. When he was home he worked at the café, while at school he experimented with a few different options. His freshmen year he worked at a local diner, initially as a part of the wait staff; management quickly recognized his talents and Jeff was soon filling in anywhere he was needed: host, cook, bottle washer, whatever had to be done. The best money, though, was from serving customers directly.

During his sophomore, year Jeff decided to try his hand at a local pizzeria. The staff split tips there, so as long as the team was firing on all cylinders he was able to do well. In the kitchen he experimented with various sauces and created some unique, tasty combination pizzas. A few of his creations remain on the menu.

Early in his junior year, as Jeff was turning twenty-one, he thought he could round out his food service education by learning the alcohol side of the business. He also reasoned that perhaps the money might be a little better. Pizza was a volume business; with decent volume they made money, but the real profits were in booze. His grandfather's café had a liquor license; Papa didn't feel a meal was complete unless it was accompanied with a proper wine. The café offered a limited selection of fine French wines and a few California options meeting Papa's discriminating standards.

Being in a college town, Jeff expected beer would dominate, but a bar and grill would allow him to learn to mix drinks while still not challenging him with to steep a learning curve – his studies always came first. Jeff spent his final two years of school working at The Thirsty Scholar. Here again he could cover all the positions, but he most enjoyed working the bar, mixing drinks and mixing it up with the regulars – mostly college students enjoying their last days of freedom.

Tonight was the final day of the fall semester. Many of the students had completed their exams earlier in the week and had headed home for winter break. The crowd at the bar tonight would be those who were not heading home, graduate students and undergrads living off campus, or those who were in no rush to get back to family confines. Many of Jeff's closest friends would be stopping by to say farewell before heading out on break.

When Jeff arrived at The Thirsty Scholar, Kim was already serving up drinks. Happy Hour would normally have been concluding at six, but this being the last Friday of the term, Happy Hour would extend until nine o'clock – the legal limit in Ohio. Steve, the owner, had stumbled onto this strategy years ago as a way to ensure he kept the college students happy and frequenting his establishment late into the term by offering cheap drinks, spicy food, and lots of fun and games. Steve, who would normally be behind the bar, was away this weekend, so the Friday night team would divide and conquer.

Kim and Annie were working the floor of the bar and grill, taking drink and food orders. Jeff was serving up the beverages at the bar and Jake was working the grill. Cyrek, a recent immigrant from Eastern Europe, was handling cleanup duty. This Thirsty Scholar Friday night crew knew how to work together and get things done. The drinks streamed, the food satisfied, and most importantly the laughs kept flowing. Life is good in a college town on a Friday night.

While most of the patrons were students, some family members, parents, and friends stopped by to catch up with buddies new and old and share the last night of college camaraderie before leaving Columbus. This mix of clientele always made for interesting and energizing conversations – exchanges Jeff relished.

By eight o'clock, the core of Jeff's tribe had assembled at the bar. They were regaling each other with war stories of trials and tribulations, cruising through and or struggling with the last hurdles of the semester: term papers, projects, and final exams. Everyone there enjoyed a collective sigh of relief – what was done was done. Only the grades were left to come, and those would be a week or so away. Now it was time to celebrate.

The annual late-fall football debate raged about the Ohio State Buckeyes and whether they would make the cut and be selected for the college championship playoffs, or have to settle for a peanuts-and-popcorn bowl game. The Buckeyes had fallen one time that season to a top-ranked team, so their future, once again, was in doubt. If you didn't know football at Ohio State, you didn't know much.

So even if they didn't *know* the game or really *care* about the game, everyone *talked* about the game.

After sports, the conversation usually turned to pop culture and celebrities. Everyone had their favorite personality mischief to share. And, as usual, the conversation would evolve toward politics. Sometimes school and local politics sparked interest, but most often national political shenanigans fueled the most emotionally charged debates.

José, a political science major, showed up just after nine, the last of Jeff's close friends to arrive. Graduating in the spring, José was ready to jump on a campaign and make a name for himself. The summer between high school and college, he served as an intern on Capitol Hill. And in the last campaign season he worked hard to help secure a seat for an up and coming freshman member to represent his home district in congress. He was willing to start at the bottom and do whatever it took to achieve fame and fortune.

Akeem, a junior, was the student athlete of the crew. A serious knee injury his freshman year kept him from the D1 squads in football and basketball at Ohio State, and also caused him to lose his athletic scholarships, but he was an all-star in the intermural leagues. Akeem was hanging in to finish his degree in business with an emphasis in marketing to get a better start on life than most of his friends back home.

Jennifer, another senior, had been one of Jeff's girlfriends earlier in college. Though their romance didn't take, Jennifer was still a good friend. She had pursued a course of study in English and was more than a little anxious about which way to go after graduation – perhaps to grad school.

10

Corrine was the sparkplug of the group. High energy, she was always going one hundred miles an hour and served as the life of the party. A junior, Corrine was studying to be an elementary school teacher. Her effervescent personality, her advanced emotional intelligence, and her cutting wit were the perfect combination for an elementary classroom.

That left Johnny and Reese. Reese, studying engineering, was the rules gal among the group. Reese pretty much kept her head down, as the engineering program was pretty demanding. A junior who had to count her pennies, Reese sought out an inexpensive, off-campus living option at the beginning of this term. She stumbled into Johnny, her polar opposite, a free-wheeling, high-energy type. Johnny had secured a tenement house unit for the year with three bedrooms and was looking for roommates. The two clicked. Johnny introduced Reese to this new group of friends. Johnny was knocking out a degree in psychology. Grades, though, weren't his main focus, as he was on an ROTC scholarship. College was more of an "experience" for Johnny. He would be joining the United States Army upon graduation and was considering making the Army a career.

Jeff's group of friends were not hard drinkers but they did enjoy each other's company. It was a lively, diverse

11

group from varied backgrounds and with varied interests. After sharing details about finals week and the usual sports and celebrity misadventures, the conversation took a turn toward the future. For most of this group of friends, one more semester and they would be launched into the real world. Were they ready? What could they expect? What options did they have?

At a biker bar you might expect patrons to compare scars and tell war stories; here at a university dive the would-be graduates compared student debt loads and employment options.

Kim, sailing around the floor taking orders and delivering drinks, was the elder of the group. Because her family was not well-to-do, and with four children in line for college, Kim's mother had researched her daughter's options and had recommended Kim serve a tour in the United States Air Force to secure the Post 9-11 GI Bill to pay for college. A few days out of high school, Kim had boarded a bus bound for the airport, and a few hours later she landed at Lackland Air Force Base in Texas for basic training. After basic and then some skills training, she completed a three-year tour of duty, assigned to Travis Air Force Base in California. As she was leaving the service and going through her transition program, the counselors and workshop facilitators recommended she focus on a course of study to optimize her professional opportunities. She decided to pick up a degree in finance. Because of her military service, Kim had zero debt and plenty of lucrative options.

Reese asked José what he was expecting to do after graduation. José outlined his path to political stardom and financial security. Reese wasn't convinced.

She queried, "You mean there's money in public service?"

"Public service? Ha! There's a misnomer if there ever was one," José pontificated with a sly smile. "Politicians only grandstand to raise money and stir the public into an emotional frenzy. Just about everything that is supposed to come from politicians or out of Washington for that matter is redacted and deemed CLASSIFIED," José emphasized. "Nothing public there. And the 'service' piece" –José feigned quotation marks in the air – "is what politics is all about. Not serving the people, but serving yourself, straining to gain more power and more money. That's the way the system works."

After a dramatic pause, José declared confidently: "And I'm going to make it work for me."

Jennifer chimed in, "A bit cynical aren't we, José?"

"No there's nothing cynical about it. I'm a realist," José smiled. "Have you ever seen a poor politician? There just aren't any."

Johnny, always one to stir the pot, fired off, "José, I've seen poor farmers…" Johnny couldn't help but chuckle, "That's right: they're dirt poor! And I've seen poor homeowners; they're house poor! And" – still on a roll – "I've seen politicians who didn't win. They're called poor losers!"

Johnny got a chuckle from everyone. Not so much from the jokes but rather for the audacity to offer such drivel.

"So there you have it. No poor 'winning' politicians," José laughed. "Look at that woman from New York: from waitress to six-figure media star over the length of a campaign. You've got to love America!"

Corrine knew José better than that, and knew he wasn't all about the money. "Come on, José, you can't seriously be that cynical about politics if you're planning on making that your life's work?"

José backed off his over-generalized position. "Alright, Corrine, you know I'm overstating it; but I have to climb out from under some serious debt. I've racked up student loans to the tune of forty thousand bucks."

"That's nothing, José," Reese rang out. "I'm from out of state. Ohio State is costing me twice as much as you. By the time I finish, which, truth be told, looks more like four more semesters, I'll have amassed about seventy thousand in debt."

"Well, at least engineering will pay the bills," Corrine countered. "I'm hoping to start in a school district that will pay down my student loans. There's no money in teaching."

Jennifer chimed in, "I don't see many good-paying prospects for English majors. I'm going to double-down and head off to graduate school. A master's degree is worth more than a bachelor's in the long run. At least that's what I'm told."

"Don't believe everything you're told, Jennifer," José chastised.

Of the eight friends, three would finish college with no debt. Kim had set herself up by serving in the military and taking advantage of the GI Bill. Johnny was heading toward military service, and Jeff had worked and saved, mostly because of his grandfather's expectations and the work ethic and practical discipline his family instilled.

José had racked up more than forty thousand in student loans. Akeem, once a promising athletic prospect deciding to go for the credentials rather than return to limited options at home, would end up twenty thousand in debt. Jennifer, whose parents had faced hard times and had gone bankrupt in 2009, were able to contribute some, but by no means were they ready to cover her entire college education. Her student debt had already accumulated to over thirty grand. Graduate school would mean digging a deeper hole.

Corrine knew teaching school wouldn't pay much, but she had faith in the system to take care of her in the end. By the time she finished her student teaching and taken the praxis to get her teaching certificate, she anticipated being nearly thirty thousand in the hole.

And Reese had chosen engineering as a practical option. She had seen her parents struggle and then split. Both were college educated but neither had focused on a field that paid. Her mom was working as an adjuster with an insurance company and her father was a manager at an auto parts store. Each had significant new family commitments. In both her mother's and her father's households, money went out as fast as it came in. For students who took on debt, which were most these days, the average college liability was running in the mid- to upper-thirty thousands. Reese was going to amass twice that much finishing her engineering degree.

"So José, who can you believe?" Corrine retorted, knowing she was fueling the fire.

"Now there's a question!" Johnny regaled. "Whom to believe?"

José was quite happy to allow Johnny to field this one. "Well, let's see," began Johnny, "my parents lied to me about Santa Claus and the Easter Bunny. And they told me I could be anything I wanted to be – all I had to do was work hard. I figured the Fine brothers had it pretty fine. I'd be just like them: post a couple of funny videos and live on Easy Street."

"How'd that work out for you?" asked Akeem.

"Well, my website has what? About three subscribers, and one of those is my mom," Johnny replied. "I'll be joining the Army at the end of the year. Not exactly Easy Street."

"Okay, so maybe our parents don't have all the answers," Corrine asserted. "But there has got to be some truth out there."

José picked up the ball. "I sat in a philosophy class this whole term. The professor talked about universal truths. "

17

The group was heading for the deep end. "From a human perspective, the professor proclaimed, almost universally, no one wants to be lied to. No one."

That sounded like a pretty powerful point to help Corrine's argument, but José continued: "But the more I thought about it, the more I realized that just isn't true. Politics is the most powerful and glaring example where people *want* to be lied to."

"What do you mean?" Akeem probed.

"Open the politician's playbook, and what do you find?" José looked around; he had his friends' attention. "You find three things: lie, cheat, and steal. Simple, straightforward, and effective."

Nobody disagreed.

"Implementing the political playbook strategy works every time," José went on. "This is what politicians do. And the public loves them for it – or rather, loves to hate them for it."

"It seems, in a perverted way, you've got something there," Jennifer admitted. "Love is not exactly the word I would use to label public sentiment, but the kiss of death for a politician is to tell the truth." Heads nodded in agreement as Jennifer continued, "Any politician who tells the truth

18

about anything of consequence can't even make a showing in a primary."

"That's right," José beamed. Jennifer was making his point. "People demand to be lied to. They vote again and again and again for the liars."

Johnny picked up and advanced the argument. "You're right, Jose, but it isn't just politicians who lie. To get attention, the media lies routinely. That's how they secure advertisers and gain influence. Government bureaucrats lie. That's how they keep their power. Business leaders lie. That's how they make their fortunes. Heck, even religious leaders lie. That's right – the same men who claim to assert moral authority. And they all cover up their lies with more lies."

Jeff, busy serving customers, was tuned into this conversation. Truth and lies were topics that had always troubled him. This discussion, which he and his friends had had many times, never ended satisfactorily.

Johnny concluded by tossing the hot potato back, "So Corrine, back to you: who can you believe?"

Corrine was on the spot, but she was ready. "Maybe it's not imperfect people we should believe, rather we should strive to adhere to certain principles."

José, genuinely curious, inquired, "And what principles might those be?"

"Freedom from bondage," Corrine asserted. "Equal rights and equal opportunity. Recognizing the dignity of all human beings."

"And don't forget," Johnny inserted, "work hard and get a good education. Just like my parents said."

"It seems like you've come back to your parents again," José ribbed and everyone laughed. "Have you got daddy issues or mommy issues?"

Akeem circled back by asking, "How does it make sense to tell everyone to work hard and get a good education, and then pile themselves up a mountain of debt to do it?"

"Akeem," responded Johnny, relishing the controversy, "piling it high is just what we do." Smiling, he continued, "Every advertisement, every utterance from a politician or journalist, and every social media maven sensationalizes the truth. They all exaggerate. They all embellish. Do you know how many times the sky has fallen and the world has ended? Nobody can keep count. Dramatizing is the American way. You're missing the key element of that adage. It's not 'Work hard and get a good education to succeed,' like most think. It's just 'work hard' – that's all."

20

Johnny made that statement with such emphasis it was as if he had sucked the air out of the room. Then he concluded, "A nice pile of debt will ensure you keep working hard. Someone else gets to enjoy the 'and succeed' part."

"Ouch!" Jennifer reprimanded. "You and José are quite the tag team. Maybe professional wrestling is in your future. You seem to be suggesting we're being set up."

"Well, aren't we?" José rang in.

Ever optimistic, Corrine offered, "We've had the opportunity to go to college. We've had the opportunity to pick up a great education. We've had opportunities many people just don't get. So we've got a little digging out to do. It could be worse."

"Does it have to be worse? Johnny countered. "Couldn't it be better?"

He left that question to sink in. The friends acknowledged the question, looked somewhat at a loss, and sipped some drinks.

Reese broke the silence and headed down a new blind alley. "What do you think of the socialist proposals all the candidates are making? Free healthcare. Free college. Guaranteed incomes. That sounds better."

Kim, keeping her pace flitting between patrons, sounded off, "Sure, it all sounds great. But in the end someone has to pay for all that supposedly free stuff."

"Well right now," Reese observed, "it looks like it's us who are paying – for just about everything."

"Look, here's what you just don't understand," José stated with authority. "Society operates by two mandates." Jose was upping the ante.

After a dramatic pause he continued, "The first: 'Might makes right.'" José let the phrase ring with some authority for a moment. "And the second: 'The many serve the few.'" Then another dramatic pause. José had this politician thing down. Then: "If you want to get ahead you must be one of the few with the might. And these days, the 'might' means 'money.' It's as simple as that."

Jeff had been listening intently, moving amongst a broad range of customer discussions. This statement from José caused him pause. "What are you saying, José? That we're not a country of laws, offering equal opportunity for all?"

"That's exactly what I'm saying, my good man," José responded confidently. "Throughout all of human history, the masses have served the few. The peasants have always served the powerful – those bold enough to seize the power.

22

Times haven't changed. Human nature hasn't changed. That we acquire debt and shackle ourselves in servitude is not by happenstance. The system always evolves to ensure the many serve the few. We just happen to be the many."

"The many with lots of debt," Jennifer observed.

Akeem smiled. "I don't like those implications."

"Maybe we could imply something else," Corrine offered hopefully.

"Such as?" José challenged.

"Look," Kim swept by, "Education and healthcare are the two fastest inflating sectors of our economy. The baby boomers are getting old, so we can expect healthcare expenditures to be rising. But with technology advancing as it is, the cost of education should be declining. Maybe José's theory holds some water."

"Sounds like cold water," Corrine suggested.

"Might makes right, and the many serve the few," Akeem summarized. "The young are rarely the mighty."

"Ah, yes, that's true," José continued building his case. "But the real problem arises when the ratio of the many relative to the few gets terribly out of whack. If you haven't noticed, money and power are concentrating in fewer and fewer hands at an accelerating rate."

"But that's the American dream," Akeem suggested. "In a land of freedom and opportunity, the many seek to become the few."

"I rest my case," José stated with confidence. And with a measure of finality he closed, "I'm not against anyone getting theirs – I'm just going to be sure to get mine."

And then, with everyone needing a little relief, the conversation turned back to lighter topics.

No real solutions, but lots of issues stuck in Jeff's brain. He'd have some things to ponder on his drive home tomorrow: truth and lies, and especially those two dictums José had theorized: **Might Makes Right** and **The Many Serve the Few**.

- 2 -

REJOICE

At a quarter 'til two, Jeff announced last call. A surprising number of patrons had stayed until closing. Being together like this was unusually special; nobody wanted to let the moment go. Finally, at closing, colleagues and kinfolk bid farewell. Most were heading home for at least some portion of the winter hiatus. Kim was from Columbus so she planned to work at The Thirsty Scholar right through break. A couple of other of Jeff's friends would hang out in Columbus before visiting family for Christmas.

In only five weeks, the gang would be back together again.

By two forty-five, Jeff was home and in bed. He set his alarm for a ten o'clock start. A quick shower, grab a breakfast bar, and he and his laundry could be on the road by ten thirty. If all went well, he would be home for lunch.

Jeff had made the drive between Columbus and Lorain countless times. He knew every curve in the highway, every stretch of construction, and every police hideaway. Rarely did he run into trouble. The distance from Columbus to Lorain was about 120 miles, mostly on Interstate 71. Just before Middleburg Heights, Jeff picked up I-80 and headed northwest.

Lorain, Ohio lay on the shores of Lake Erie, thirty miles west of Cleveland. Times weren't great, and Lorain suffered many of the same economic and social challenges as Cleveland. Once a manufacturing hub, home to plants run by American Ship Building, Ford, and United States Steel, Lorain had become a de-industrialized relic with few opportunities and a declining population. As Lorain lost manufacturing, prospects in Cleveland became more valuable, but Cleveland too faltered. And Cleveland's struggles weighed on the people of Lorain. As when good times spread and lifted spirits across the region, tough times extended like a plague, and nobody was immune.

It was a sunny, crisp day in central Ohio. Jeff knew to beat traffic he needed to start early, launching late morning wasn't optimal, but at least cruising with traffic at highway speed on a Saturday morning gave him plenty of time to think.

As was his habit, Jeff listened to classic rock on the drive. He knew just where to switch between stations. He grew up listening to "oldies" of the 70s and 80s – his mother's and his aunt's favorites. Queen, The Rolling Stones, Styx, Bruce Springsteen, and Boston were balanced by the likes of the Bee Gees, John Denver, and ABBA. These classics were a taste of home.

Upon rolling out of Columbus, Jeff's mind soon wandered back to José's comments the previous evening. **Might Makes Right.** and **The Many Serve the Few.** Jeff could see the obvious utility or reality in those dictums, but were they as all-encompassing of human society as José had declared?

The United States, after all, was a nation founded on ideals, or more accurately, principles. Americans had never fully realized those ideals or fully embodied those principles, but nevertheless they inspired progress.

The idea of a society founded on life affirming, achievement-oriented principles drew people from around the globe ready and willing to work. Melding together, they built an immigrant nation. Freedom and opportunity were enticing offerings. America was the one place on earth – or at least strived to be the one place – where origin didn't matter. What mattered was the contribution you made and the people you served. A nation committed to the rule of law allowed everyone to avail themselves of the ultimate gift: opportunity. And in America, that opportunity had blossomed into unparalleled prosperity.

Could it be that mankind's true nature – to strive for power above all else, and the right of might – would topple the great American experiment, the once fabled dream of freedom and opportunity in this land of many blessings? This idea troubled Jeff as he rolled down the highway.

Jeff made good time. Soon he was coasting down the Lorain Boulevard exit off of I-80. He crossed over I-90 and headed into town. Two more miles and he turned left at Oakwood Park onto East 36th. Driving by the park reminded Jeff of his great neighborhood friends and all the adventures only children enjoy. A right after the park and one more left, and Jeff was home.

Jeff's was a working class neighborhood. No fancy houses here, just comfortable, solid good old American craftsmanship. Most of the homes were built in the 1950s and 60s when manufacturing was king. The prosperous days of high wages and full employment were long gone, but the residents were still making the best of it. Most of the homes and grounds were tidy and well kept. When dire times befell some unfortunate neighbor and a property was abandoned,

28

the abutting residents made it their mission to keep up appearances. They would cut the grass and trim the bushes until the bankers and local authorities could sort out the status of the real estate and allow it to change hands.

Jeff's house was similar to what East Coasters would label a tenement house. Originally built as an upscale, for the neighborhood, single-family home, Papa had bought the house fourteen years before. Jeff's father, a fire fighter, had been killed battling an industrial blaze; Papa orchestrated the real estate shuffle to ensure finances did not become an issue. Multiple families, or in this case an extended family, living under one roof made more financial sense then keeping several residences.

Papa had lived above the bakery and café since he started that business fifty-five years before. He owned the building outright. Papa turned the café apartment over to his other daughter, Janice, and her family. Janice was that aunt who ran the bakery and café now in partnership with Jeff's mom Lizzie. Papa and Lizzie divided their house into two comfortable units, one for Papa and the other for Lizzie, Jeff, and Jeff's sister Jess, short for Jessica.

When Jeff pulled into the driveway in the back of the house, Jess popped out the back door to greet him.

"Welcome home!"

"Thanks, Jess. Good to see you."

"How was the drive?"

"Uneventful, as usual. An opportunity to ponder."

"Sometimes I think you think too much," said Jess.

"Well," replied Jeff, "I'd rather be accused of thinking too much than of thinking too little."

"I'm not so sure about that." Jess nudged skeptically with a smile on her face.

Jeff and Jess grabbed Jeff's bags – mostly laundry – and headed for the house. Sitting in the window, closely watching Jeff's arrival, was Princess Grace. Gracie, as she was affectionately called was a rambunctious, young, white Ragdoll cat. Gracie was a fixture of the household. At about two years old, she had the energy of a kitten. She particularly enjoyed stirring things up when the household grew too quiet – usually early mornings. And with Jeff home, that meant more options to command attention. Everyone loved Princess Grace. Jeff put down his bags and picked up Gracie immediately upon entering. True to her ragdoll nature, Gracie went limp in Jeff's arms and purred her warm welcome.

"She missed you," Jess observed. "Mom is on her way from the café. Based on your departure text, we figured you'd arrive around twelve-thirty. Aunt Janice is on today, but mom was helping with the Saturday morning rush. She wanted to get home to have lunch with you here."

As Jess spoke mom's car pulled into the driveway. "And look, here she comes."

Hugs and kisses followed. Though they had seen Jeff at Thanksgiving a few weeks before, the end of the term marked a turning point. Jeff was closing in on his goal and Lizzie was anticipating significant changes ahead. Jeff would be graduating in the spring and Jess would be heading off to college in the fall. Mom wasn't sure she was ready for such potentially drastic changes. Gracie would be lonely too. Of course Gracie would have Madeleine, Papa's little dog, to play with.

Jeff's mom's name was Olivia. This was also Lizzie's mother's name. Rather than refer to two Olivias, the family immediately established the affectionate Lizzie substitute. Lizzie whipped up Jeff's favorite for lunch: tomato soup, homemade and ready for the occasion, accompanied by a three-cheese grilled cheese – with bacon, of course – on fresh baked sourdough bread. The family were bakers, after

31

all. That lunch standard was a nostalgic and comforting welcome home.

Lively lunch conversation covered the obligatory term-completion progress reports for both students. How did it all go? And how did each of them think they were doing?

Jeff, for his part, was satisfied with his progress. His ultimate goal was to complete college in four years with something better than a 3.0 GPA. He was tracking near a 3.35 if all went as expected. Jess, a senior Titan at Lorain High School, was on the fast track academically. Jess had enrolled in Titan College early on, and had been completing college-level courses throughout her high school career. If all went according to plan, she would receive her associate of science degree along with her high school diploma in the spring. Then it was off to nursing school. Again, a prospect Lizzie welcomed but did not look forward to.

The discussion then circled back to important home-based prospects. How were things at the bakery and café going? How were Aunt Janice, Uncle Bill, and Cousin Jackie doing? And of course, how was Papa?

Papa would have been there for Jeff's homecoming lunch, but he had an event he was helping to set up for that evening at the café. The café normally closed at seven, but today the café would close at six to host a special event. It was the Wexler's sixtieth wedding anniversary. Mr. Wexler was one of Papa's oldest and dearest friends. Fittingly, as "*wexler*" was the Germanic form of "moneychanger," Mr. Wexler was the banker who helped a young immigrant establish a thriving bakery and café in a small but growing city back in the 1960s. It was one of Mr. Wexler's first projects as a bank loan officer. Papa and Mr. Wexler grew up professionally together as the best of friends. After lunch and a few chores around the house Jeff, Jess, and Lizzie would be heading to the café to lend a hand preparing for the anniversary celebration.

At three, Lizzie zipped over to the café to help with food preparation. Jeff and Jess showed up a little after four. Closing at six for a party at seven meant a speedy transition. And the usual Saturday afternoon pastry orders had to be filled. Papa never opened the café on Sundays; he declared, "Sunday is the Lord's day – a day of thanksgiving, reflection and rest." Patrons of the bakery and café learned long ago to order and pick up Sunday breads and treats late on Saturday, as baking went on all day.

As the afternoon meal service was still going on, Papa had three major items to orchestrate. They were expecting

33

anniversary celebration guests to begin showing up at about six thirty. Food had to be prepared with a synchronized serving at seven fifteen; the café dining room had to be rearranged to ensure the focal point was on the guests of honor; and decorations had to be placed and hung. Papa knew, as the Wexlers were in their eighties, the entire event had to move along to ensure everyone made it home for lights-out by ten o'clock. In concert with Janice, Papa had a plan wired, and Lizzie and Jeff, Jess, Jackie, and the café staff were all in support.

Janice and the usual Saturday team handled the afternoon diners and the Sunday pastry order rush. Papa and Lizzie busied themselves preparing food for the party, which left Jeff, Jess, and Jackie (Janice's daughter) to coordinate decorations and room set up. The team worked like a well-oiled machine – they had done this before for other special events – and had everything beautifully decorated and in place as the first guests arrived.

Papa and Janice had planned every detail, even ensuring everyone had their Sunday best clothing upstairs in Janice's apartment, so that as soon as preparations were set each member of the family could run up and change. Papa, as usual, looked smart in his double-breasted vintage suit – the perfect attire for this seminal event.

The Wexlers, though not as active as they once were, still had many friends in town. The café was filled to capacity. Wonderful toasts, great food, fine wine, laughter, and reminiscent tears punctuated the evening. Everything went according to plan.

Jeff, circulating throughout the room assisting with food service, watched guest interactions and marveled at the genuine respect, admiration, and affection freely expressed and exchanged. Jeff realized these strong bonds and heartfelt relationships were rare and exceptional indeed these days. No one in attendance seemed to jockey for status or dominance. No one tried to steal attention away from the Wexlers. Everyone celebrated, remembered, and rejoiced. New acquaintances became friends, while old friends embraced, reflected on past adventures, and recounted tales of mishap, mischief, and merriment. Laughter echoed throughout the café. Neighbors, professional colleagues, church and community leaders, and friends welcomed one another with genuine enthusiasm.

Everyone attending the anniversary party focused on coming together, sharing and celebrating. This affection and sentiment stood against and very far removed from José's declaration that people were driven by the adage, Might Makes Right. Jeff was energized to see and feel the unpretentious esteem and sincere caring – the love – animating that room. People who cared about one another, and who cared about their community could live by another dictum, a better dictum – a more powerful principle. Jeff knew he had to dig deeper.

By nine fifteen, festivities were winding down. The Wexlers sat at the door of the café bidding fond farewells to all the family members and friends who had come by to mark their sixty years together.

Papa and Janice, sticklers for detail, even had a post-party exit plan. Papa played the role of distinguished host, as nearly all of the Wexler's guests were his friends too. If a guest hadn't been before tonight, they were Papa's friends now.

Papa spoke six languages fluently: French, English, Spanish, Italian, German, and Polish. Papa's father, Jeff's great grandfather, had been a language teacher back in Papa's native France. With a natural knack for languages and over sixty years serving customers in this diverse community, Papa could at least manage to get by in almost every language heard in the café.

Janice and the kitchen and wait staff – long-time employees who enjoyed the occasional overtime event – cleaned and organized, while Jeff, Jess, and Jackie shuttled gifts, flowers, and some leftovers into the Wexler family's cars to ensure everything made it home. More decorations, picture albums with updates, and a few other memorabilia would follow a couple days later when Papa made his usual Monday afternoon visits. Jeff, of course, would help and make sure those follow-on items were transferred as well.

In accordance with the master plan, the Wexlers were gone by nine-forty and the café doors were locked by ten. Everything was mostly ready for the Monday early morning bakery start at four o'clock. Janice would likely knock out any overlooked details during her habitual Sunday evening sweep of the café.

Jess rode with Lizzie and Papa rode with Jeff on the drive home. Jeff and Papa hadn't really had the time to focus on Jeff's homecoming as the anniversary event had kept the family hopping. Papa was tired, thrilled for a number of reasons, and satisfied that despite a few minor complications everything had come together and the Wexler's got the recognition they deserved. Now it was time to focus on his grandson.

Jeff and Jess both possessed extraordinary language skills. They grew up speaking French and English at home. At Papa's urging, Jeff went on to master Spanish and other Romance languages as well. His fluency in Spanish was one of the reasons he and José had become such good friends. Jess, a bit of a "free-thinker," looked down the road and so turned her attention to mastering Chinese, with a special focus on Mandarin and Cantonese. Almost anyone who walked into the bakery and café could speak to someone on the staff in their native tongue.

As Papa and Jeff settled in the car, they conversed in French.

"Jeff, I don't know what we would have done without you," Papa began. "Thanks for all your help today."

"If I didn't know better, Papa," smiled Jeff, "I would have thought you scheduled the end of my semester to exactly coincide with the Wexler's anniversary."

"I think you're on to me, Jeff." Papa patted Jeff's shoulder and then added, "It's great to have you home."

"It's great to be home, Papa. How have you been?"

"Well, other than my knees giving me a little trouble and my cribbage game slipping a bit, I think all is going pretty well." Papa was never one to complain, but he always tried to be honest and genuine. "So what are your big plans for your last winter break?"

"No real big plans," replied Jeff. "I'm thinking this may likely be my last long stint at home, so I just thought I'd contribute at the café and enjoy my time with family and friends."

"Sounds like a great plan to me," said Papa, relaxing in his seat. "Maybe a little cribbage tomorrow?"

"You bet, Papa. Now, you said you're slipping a bit," Jeff then asked with a smile, "so should I be worried you're trying to set me up?"

"We'll just have to see tomorrow, now won't we?" Papa replied with a hint of mischief in his voice and a twinkle in his eye.

The distance from the café to home was less than four miles. The two did not have much time together but they each cherished every moment. It was after ten, which was Papa's usual lights out time, so Jeff wished Papa a good night's sleep and confirmed a meeting time of four in the afternoon for a resumption of their long-standing cribbage

39

match. Jeff figured that once he got on a winning roll –
assuming that ever happened – it would take him a few years
to make up the win-loss deficit he had built up over more
than a decade of challenging Papa. But cribbage with Papa
was never really about winning; although Papa might see
things differently, the game was an opportunity to spend
time together.

Jeff, Jess, and Lizzie wound down the evening
reminiscing about reconnecting with the Wexlers and their
guests. The three went their separate ways just before
midnight; they had to be ready to collect Papa and make the
eight-thirty Sunday mass.

For most of his adult life, Papa had been a member of the
Nativity of the Blessed Virgin Mary Parish, a worship
community with Polish-American roots. The Nativity parish
was nearest the café, and the Polish-American community
welcomed a young French immigrant with open arms. When
Papa moved with Lizzie toward the east side of town after
Jeff's father died, he felt it was his duty to switch parishes
and join the local congregation. Papa often attended daily
mass at the Nativity and was still quite active in that
community. Jeff, his parents, and sister had been members of
what in 2010 evolved into Saint Frances Xavier Cabrini

40

Parish. Papa felt he made a timely transition, as Saint Frances Xavier Cabrini was the patron saint of immigrants. Papa had immigrated to America in 1945 at the age of nine.

The readings and sermon that Sunday had an Advent – Christmas preparation – theme. As it was the third week of Advent, Gaudete or Rejoice Sunday, the single pink candle on the Advent wreath was lit. The readings came from the *Book of Isaiah, Paul's First Letter to the Thessalonians,* and from the *Gospel of John.* The priest, Father Joseph, was a master of translating the themes of the readings into relevant and timely stories to motivate and stir the congregation.

Jeff particularly liked when a priest came out from the pulpit, as was Father Joseph's practice, and told personal stories to engage believers. A preacher who could connect with his congregation emotionally and spiritually was a rare and sought after talent. The people of Saint Frances Xavier Cabrini knew they were lucky to have Father Joseph.

Father Joseph, ever enthusiastic and upbeat – rare qualities in a priest – weaved the words of Isaiah, Paul, and John into a tale from his youth, something he experienced in a far-off land, a saga which felt eerily relevant to America today.

"I had recently completed infantry training at Fort Benning, Georgia. I joined the Army to escape small town life in rural Indiana." Father Joseph smiled at his parishioners. "You know what I mean." The parishioners smiled back.

"I wanted to go on an adventure, see the world, and begin to make my mark in it. I was young, energetic, and idealistic. Growing up in rural Indiana, I wasn't quite ready for what I faced when I graduated boot camp and shipped off to Europe.

"It was late 1995. The former Republic of Yugoslavia, comprised of competing ethnic groups unified by a strong man after World War II, dictator Josip Tito, had been thrown into political and social turmoil with the collapse of the Soviet Union in 1989. The unrest amongst the various groups rose beyond partisan politics to outright civil war." He stressed the word civil, feigning quotation marks in the air. "A contradiction if there ever was one. After Yugoslavia disintegrated, nationalists were elected and assumed power. Distrust, which had stewed for generations, surfaced amongst long-standing adversaries. A perceived power vacuum opened, which all sides seized upon as a window of opportunity. The ensuing conflict presented the ugliest face of man.

"Ethnicity undergirded by contrived religious components drove both sides to commit heinous, barbarous acts. The combatants rationalized and rallied around notions of religious fealty, family, and community loyalty. They determined to eliminate what they labeled a heathen threat before their own existence was put at risk."

Jeff could feel passion rising from within Father Joseph as he relived his experience; he seemed overcome with a combination of compassion and repulsion.

"The truth behind the smokescreen of justifications was simply hatred and animosity," said Father Joseph. "The real issues were not religious, nor were they about establishing a fair or fruitful political and economic system. The murder and mayhem were acts of vengeance – power-plays to establish dominance and gain control."

Jeff thought to himself, here's that theme again.

Father Joseph continued, "There is no such thing as a religious war. True religion is a path to spiritual understanding and the unbounded love of God." He then gazed up at the crucifix hanging over the altar. "War is always about power, pure and simple. Who is going to wield

43

power." He paused for dramatic effect. Every eye was transfixed on him. You could hear a pin drop, the people in the pews were so quiet.

"The hatred and violence in the former Yugoslavia was an unleashing of men's worst passions." His tone and posture then softened. "Now I've set a pretty horrific scene here on this Rejoice Sunday. War in Yugoslavia. More than one hundred and fifty thousand men, women, and children perished unnecessarily at the hands of vindictive, spiteful, hate-filled men. Men who had been neighbors, colleagues, perhaps even friends, just months before. How could such hatred have taken hold?"

Father Joseph surveyed the faces in the pews. Each person wondered…

"I see you're questioning: 'This is nothing to rejoice about. Why are you taking us here?' You'll see." He added with a wry grin. "After years of bloodshed and fighting, the United Nations finally acted, and in 1995 got the belligerent parties to sign what was called the Dayton Peace Accords. The United Nations sent a peacekeeping force into Bosnia. Those peacekeepers were led by soldiers from the United States.

"I was one of those soldiers. I went into Bosnia in early 1996. It was cold and wet and miserable. We were not there to impose an end to hostilities. No, we were there to maintain a tenuous and fragile peace. I can tell you, I was anxious from the very first moment. I didn't know what to expect as we advanced into that war-torn country. We weren't sure if we were going to be well received or if we were in for a fight. But I clung to those words of scripture, 'Do not quench the Spirit... test everything; and hold fast to what is good.'

"Traveling across the countryside, I saw firsthand what hate had wrought. It was incredibly sad and incredibly disturbing to see the destruction and the evidence of slaughter consummated on such a scale. This had obviously been a beautiful country, inhabited by beautiful people. It was now torn asunder by hate-filled passions.

"Every day, for months on end, we saw the dirty, weary faces of men, women, and children who had endured horrible conditions and the most brutal and violent actions of men."

His tone now turned positive for the first time since he began his homily as he asked, "But you know what else we saw?" He paused. "I was serving as part of a security detail supporting a civil affairs detachment. That detachment had a local Serbian interpreter assigned to it. I became fast friends with that interpreter. We remain friends to this day. As we traveled around that former war zone and interacted with more and more people, we began to see signs of hope on what had been desperate and forlorn faces.

"While the distrust of former neighbors subsided only bitterly, painfully slowly," he stressed those words, "the locals put their hope and trust in us – men and women from a nation half a world away. Our being there for them, meant hope was still alive. They didn't look at us as conquerors or victors; those people who had suffered so much saw us as a glimmer of salvation. America was a legendary beacon of hope and a nation of principle, and its soldiers were champions of truth. They saw us as offering them an opportunity to begin again on a better path.

"I spent a year there in Bosnia. It was a challenging year. I was just a junior soldier – a kid – doing what I was told to do, and doing what I could. We kept watch. We patrolled. We separated belligerent parties. We calmed passions. We played with children. We helped out the elderly and sick as best we could. We began to rebuild trust, and lives, and finally communities.

"My service in Bosnia, as a soldier, changed me; and the direction of my life. We were not perfect. We were not

46

saintly. I was not so bold as to pray without ceasing and give thanks in all circumstances. But I did what I could, and what I had to do. And slowly peace returned as the Muslims and Christians, Serbs and Slovaks, Croatians and Albanians, and others began to reestablish relationships by rebuilding a foundation of trust.

"But that is neither the end nor the point of my tale. No, because you see," Father Joseph raised his finger as his eyes lit up, "Isaiah proclaimed, 'God will cause righteousness and praise to spring up before all the nations.' And Paul exhorted, 'Pray without ceasing, give thanks in all circumstances… Do not quench the Spirit… but test everything; and hold fast to what is good.'

"You see, now, these days, some thirty years after hostilities began – when selfish men committed brazen, thoughtless and horrific acts – God is moving hearts to change." Genuine enthusiasm flowed from Father Joseph. "I spoke to my friend, that interpreter I had mentioned, just this week. He told me about a miracle that is happening. Veterans of the Yugoslavia or Bosnia Wars, as they were known, are men who have faced widespread censure, not unlike the blame cast on veterans here in the United States returning from Vietnam. Political leaders across the former

Yugoslav Republic effectively played the blame game, indicting perpetrators from neighboring states as the culpable parties to wartime atrocities. Those who eventually claimed power distanced themselves from that war, any responsibility for carnage, and from men who once fought for what they thought was right.

"After decades of regret, many veterans – men once driven by ethnic hatred – suffered from physical, psychological, and — most detrimentally – spiritual wounds. Many who lived in poverty, carrying substantial debt, and receiving little or no support or services, took their own lives. They felt they had nowhere to turn for relief from their misery and regret."

Father Joseph's story was coming together. "The Lord God will cause righteousness and praise to spring up before all the nations. Rejoice always. Pray without ceasing. Even in suffering give thanks. Give thanks in all circumstances."

Father Joseph looked each man, woman and child in the eye. His passion and conviction were palpable. "Those men, lost and without hope, began reaching out. My interpreter friend told me how those long-suffering victims of war – of hatred and ambition – are now reaching out for consolation, reconciliation, and forgiveness."

This is why Father Joseph intended his flock to rejoice. "This reaching out; this breaking of barriers; this opening of hearts is the work of God! The Holy Spirit is stirring within the hearts of men, former combatants and enemies, the sentiment and power of healing. Former opponents are brought together by common wounds.

"Healing and forgiving are not easy. Veterans expose themselves to social censure and ridicule by admitting they participated in a war all would just as soon forget. But the wounds persist. Without forgiveness and without healing, the hatred and the divide persist. But with God's guidance and healing touch, these men are finding a better way. Openness and humility are the way to forgiveness. And forgiveness leads back to the light and joy of Jesus Christ."

Father Joseph was rejoicing now, and his joy was spreading. "Men in the formerly war-torn Yugoslavia are engaging in small, painful steps to welcome in the healing hand of our Father. John came as a witness to testify to the light, so that all might believe through Him." He waved his hand, drawing every listener into his message. "The pain of those who suffer cause voices to cry out in the wilderness. Make straight the way of the Lord. For kindness and compassion are what God showers on all of us.

49

"We are called to cry out; to make straight the way of the Lord.

"We are called to see the humanity in one another – the face of God in our brother and sister."

Father Joseph looked at select parishioners, then to their left and right. "And we are called to rejoice. Rejoice that Jesus Christ has brought you to this day – to the opportunity of a lifetime.

"Make straight the way of the Lord."

This was Father Joseph at his best.

"You, me, we – all of us have the opportunity to live and to love. We have the opportunity to explore and experience, learn and grow, create and contribute. It is God that gives us that opportunity. Rejoice in this. If men who were swept up in a grievous war can, by the grace of God, find healing, then we can rejoice and find love in whatever trials we must endure.

"God will cause righteousness and praise to spring up before all the nations. Christ's healing hand touches us all. Pray without ceasing, give thanks in all circumstances. Do not quench the Spirit; test everything and hold fast to what is good. You are called as a witness to testify to the light, so

50

that all might believe through Him. Make straight the way of the Lord. Rejoice."

The contagion of Father Joseph's enthusiasm radiated throughout the church. Being there, then, Jeff found just what he needed that morning.

After mass, Jeff, Papa, Lizzie, and Jess mingled with the other parishioners in the commons. They shared coffee and pastry – fine treats from a local French café, courtesy of Papa and Lizzie – and caught up on the week's happenings. As Jeff hadn't been seen since Thanksgiving, he had more catching up to do.

Once the socializing wound down, the quartet headed home. It was time to prepare Sunday brunch, a long-standing family tradition. Papa went off into his apartment to change clothes and read a little scripture before joining the others at about a quarter after eleven. Jeff and Jess joined Lizzie in their kitchen. Each had a role to play in brunch preparations.

The three engaged in lively conversation as they cooked and readied the table. Father Joseph's homily was a powerful point of discussion, as were some contentious points of local, state, and national politics.

When the conversation turned to politics, Jeff brought up the Friday night banter amongst his friends at The Thirsty

51

Scholar. Lizzie and Jess knew José quite well, as he was a long-time college friend of Jeff's. José had been to the house a number of times. Jeff shared that he was troubled by the gravity of what José had asserted: Might Makes Right, and the Many Serve the Few. The statements seemed accurate and descriptive of historical conditions. But, as Jeff expressed, "Those dictates were what a free and equal society were supposed to overcome. And instead of overcoming, 'we the people' are becoming more enslaved." Lizzie and Jess recognized Jeff's genuine concern.

"Jeff, you should talk to Papa about this," Lizzie suggested. "I know he'll have a perspective on those statements. The attempted exercise of might, to get the many to serve the few, is how we ended up here as Americans. Papa will have lots to share."

Then the conversation turned away from such weighty topics and settled back on holiday preparations. Soon enough, Papa entered through the kitchen door. "I smell some goodies cooking," he said. "Who's ready to eat?"

Just then the doorbell rang. The Hargraves – Bob, Lori, and their twin daughters, Lisa and Joan –were at the door. Lori had her signature egg casserole in hand. Lizzie invited a neighbor family to every Sunday brunch. Bob and Lori had settled in this neighborhood a few months before Papa found his place. Bob and Lori had actually mentioned to Papa, at the café, that the house Jeff now lived in was coming on the market.

Lisa and Joan were born two years after Jeff's family had moved in. As Jess was five years older than the twins, she was groomed for babysitting duty from the start. Lisa and Joan were like younger siblings in Jeff's family. The truth was that everyone Papa met was family. That's what Lizzie, Jess, and Jeff had always known.

Hugs and kisses all around. The eight enjoyed a delectable brunch together. They shared lots of laughs as each in turn recollected interesting and engaging circumstances at school and work. Papa liked to keep things light, especially when children were around. He felt there was already enough conflict in the world. Rehashing or reliving it was rarely worth the effort. Not that Papa didn't like difficult or deep conversations; he just preferred to deal with weightier subjects when the mood was right.

At twelve forty-five, Papa stood up from the table to excuse himself. "Nap time," he declared.

Everyone, including Lisa and Joan, were familiar with the routine. Papa made his way around the table sharing affectionate hugs and kisses with each family member, and guests were considered family members too. As he made his way to the door, Papa turned to Jeff and said, "Cribbage at four?"

Jeff responded, "You bet, Papa. I'm ready for you today."

After smiling a big, warm smile, Papa waved and headed out the door. "We'll see."

The rest of the crew began to clean up. Once the table was clean and the dishes were loaded into the dishwasher, the Hargraves bid a warm farewell. This was the best way to spend a Sunday – quality time with dear friends and family.

- 3 -

SHEEP, HERDERS, AND WOLVES

At four, Jeff knocked twice on Papa's doorframe, as was his custom, before entering Papa's apartment. It was like stepping back in time – a time Jeff very much relished.

Papa was not one for extravagances. His apartment was adorned with much of his original furniture, acquired in the late fifties and sixties. Papa's wife, Jeff's grandmother Olivia, had chosen most of the pieces; and since her passing, twenty years before, Papa preferred to cherish the memories and keep things pretty much the same.

When Papa moved from over the café to this unit, Lizzie and Janice had managed to re-stuff and re-upholster the living room set and his easy chair, but Papa insisted on subdued colors, mostly greys and browns, like the originals. Olivia had, over the years, taken to add splashes of color with throws and pillows, to keep things vibrant and fresh. Lizzie and Janice continued the tradition.

Jeff was fond of the antique pieces of furniture: the heavy mahogany hutch serving as a makeshift liquor cabinet, the giant polished wood wardrobe, the vintage grandfather clock, and that huge what Jeff called a "sea-chest" filled with old pictures, newspaper clippings, and other memorabilia.

One of Jeff's earliest memories, from when he was four or five, was of hiding in that chest. Papa had it cleaned out then. It was Jeff's favorite hiding place, and Papa pretended for the longest time, again and again, to never suspect Jeff was hiding, crouched, in that chest.

Papa even had an old-fashioned, vintage 1960s turntable and vinyl record collection. Since vinyl was making a comeback, Papa insisted he was avant-garde and on the cutting edge when it came to music.

Papa's collection consisted of mostly classics including Bach, Mozart, Beethoven, and of course the French composer Claude Debussy. Debussy's non-traditional style led Papa to American icons like Irving Berlin and Duke Ellington. To diversify his collection, Papa compiled a grand selection of big band sounds and more than a few albums of the great crooners like Frank Sinatra and Nat King Cole.

Jeff remembered vividly many an afternoon spent playing cribbage with Papa, discussing deep and far-reaching philosophical issues and solving life's not so far-reaching but at the time seemingly intractable problems. The intractable issues usually involved school challenges or girls. During all those fireside conversations and chats, sometimes soothing, sometimes invigorating sounds reverberated in the background. This, to Jeff, was the safest place on earth.

Papa was the most well-read and informed person Jeff ever conversed with. Papa was wise in ways Jeff never experienced with anyone else.

Papa's father had been a language teacher who loved learning. Papa's father would tell his young son, "Understanding the language, the words, the context, and the meaning, is ninety percent of the battle." That love of learning, of trying to see with a broad view and with understanding, continued through the generations.

Though he possessed little formal education, Papa was more knowledgeable than most. He devoured books, newspapers, and any useful information he could get his hands on. He had studied all the classics, and even now, well into his eighties, was up to date on emerging technologies. As time seemed to be accelerating, Papa became more of a rock, embodying standards and principled convictions keeping civility alive in an increasingly uncivil world.

Papa's dog Madeleine greeted Jeff at the door. No longer a spring chicken, she felt it was her duty, truly her obligation, to greet every visitor, and to collect a nice scratch or affectionate pat for her efforts, and maybe even a treat. Jeff knew were Papa kept a stash of treats just behind the door. Jeff was one of Madeleine's favorite guests.

A Maltese mix, Madeleine was a rescue, as all Papa's dogs had been. Soon after Papa and Olivia married, Olivia convinced Papa to take in the last of a café customer's Scottish terrier mix puppies. Olivia dubbed that puppy Éclair, after the French pastry. Éclair became the café dog. Every dog Papa owned since had been named after a French pastry.

Papa had a fire burning in the fireplace. The crackling of dry hardwood and the sweet smell of maple hung in the air. Jeff could feel the warmth as he approached.

"*Bonjour,* Jefferson!"

"*Salut,* Papa! *Comment allez-vous*?"

"*Trés bien,* Jefferson."

Papa preferred to sit in a rocker near the fireplace for cribbage matches in the winter. A fine wine, radiant warmth, and an engaging conversation were like heaven for Papa. Jeff's seat was on the couch next to a blanket, which was Madeleine's preferred perch. Madeleine followed a habitual route up onto the fireplace hearth, across a ramp to an end table, and then onto the couch. The cards, the cribbage board, and cheese and crackers were already set on the coffee table.

One last detail had to be attended to.

The afternoon conversation continued in French. Papa inquired, "What are you in the mood for today?"

Jeff knew exactly what that meant. "As you say Papa, 'A good red always invites in a fine afternoon.'"

"I was hoping you'd say that. I've had my eye on this 2014 Georges de Latour Cabernet Sauvignon, and I thought your return home would be the perfect opportunity to try it."

Papa took his wine and his cribbage very, very seriously.

"It is not the Médoc of Bordeaux but Napa Valley. If you'll indulge me, I hope it lives up to its reputation and proves fitting for such an auspicious occasion as the completion of your penultimate semester."

"Ah, Papa, you flatter me. Whatever you choose will be the perfect selection."

Papa usually drank fifty-dollar bottles of wine. The retail on this cabernet was better than one hundred and forty dollars. He really was breaking out the good stuff, Jeff thought to himself. I wonder what he will open for graduation?

"Now it is you who flatter me," Papa replied as he reached for the corkscrew to uncork the cabernet. Both Papa and Jeff's attention then turned to the game.

Cribbage, a card game designed traditionally for two players, can be played by four or more. Over the years Papa, Janice, Jackie, and Jess had engaged in some epic cribbage matches; the four of them were expecting to light-heartedly battle again over this holiday break.

In cribbage, players earn points by grouping various combinations of cards and achieving predetermined point values during card play, aiming at point totals of fifteen and thirty-one; and then counting points in each player's hand and the crib. Game play usually takes about thirty minutes, but a game can be won on the deal. Papa and Jeff's tradition had always been to play a match – the best two out of three games. Jeff was so far behind in match victories he had lost count. But competing was not why he played; being there and spending time with Papa was reason enough.

As the game proceeds, the score is kept by advancing pegs along a cribbage board. Playing as frequently as they did, cards aged, were discarded, and replaced, but Jeff and Papa's matches always were scored on Papa's antique board.

Papa had been given his cribbage board as a gift from a merchant marine sailor he had met while he was "crossing the pond" – the Atlantic Ocean – emigrating to America at the conclusion of World War II. Because he was traveling by himself and able to speak several languages, the crew took a liking to the affable young French boy. Sailors taught Papa to play cribbage. One sailor handed Papa that board as he started down the gangplank in the port of Montreal, Canada, where a new life awaited. Cribbage became one of Papa's many passions, and that board became one of Papa's most prized possessions.

As a young boy in France, Papa had experienced heartache and loss. In 1940, the Nazis invaded France and occupied Paris. Throughout Europe, times were tough for many, most especially the Jews.

Papa's younger sister, Elise, was born in 1941; she barely survived three years, dying of scarlet fever, a bacterial illness caused by strep. Papa's mother was never the same after losing beautiful, precious Elise. At Papa's age, he didn't completely understand what his parents faced, but he sensed their pain and grief. And he missed his baby sister.

Months after his sister's death, Papa's father, Louis, died assisting Allied paratroopers during the Normandy landings in early June 1944. Papa was eight years old. Papa's mother survived the war but struggled with illness – really a broken heart – in that dry summer of 1945. After Papa's father was killed, his mother's condition grew increasingly dire. Relatives put Papa on a transport vessel to live "temporarily" with an aunt and uncle in Montreal, Quebec, the French-speaking province of Canada.

That aunt and uncle, Claire and Marcel, had fled France when the specter of Hitler began to emerge in Germany. Marcel, Papa's father's brother, had fought in the last year of The Great War – the war to end all wars, that didn't. Marcel saw the writing on the wall and tried to convince Papa's father, Louis, to start a new life in Canada. Louis was too young to experience The Great War and so did not feel the same trauma and foreboding threat as Marcel. Louis was sustaining the family traditions there in the Normandy region of France, teaching school and making a contribution.

Claire and Marcel had moved to Montreal in the midst of the Great Depression. They rented a modest apartment and found work, but they aspired to something more. They never had children of their own, but welcomed Papa with open arms when he joined them in Montreal at the age of nine.

That following summer, 1946, Papa got word his mother
had died. He always regretted not being able to attend her
funeral. Marcel was one to say engagement was the best
distraction, and in that summer of '46 he saw an opportunity.
Claire and Marcel and a young Papa relocated to Lorain,
Ohio, a city named for the Lorraine region of France. As
Claire, Marcel, and young Papa soon discovered, the
Lorraine region was a region the Germans too once claimed.
There were far more Germans in Lorain, Ohio than French,
but the three settled in and began to build a new life.

On that Sunday afternoon, Papa and Jeff focused on the
game play. As they sipped that crisp cabernet, the
conversation revisited some ground from the previous
evening and from morning brunch. Sometimes it's hard to
keep up with all the details, especially when engaging with
so many people so quickly. Papa explained the particulars of
the happenings in the lives of many of the folks Jeff was
curious about from those recent conversations.

Soon enough, the first cribbage game drew to a close.
Papa somehow had managed, as he normally did, to surge to
a lead. He then played an eight, setting up a run. At that
point, Jeff didn't have many options. He secured two points
for the fifteen, but sure enough Papa made the run, then

counted his hand, and just like that Papa was at one hundred twenty-one. Game over. One game for Papa, none for Jeff.

Madeleine shifted her position on the blanket. It seemed she knew this pattern well.

Jeff got up to pour some more wine, grab some more crackers and cheese, and tend to the fire. Papa had some unusually tasty cheese selections today.

As the second, and potentially deciding, game began, Papa asked about José and Jeff's other classmates. Jeff steered the conversation to what had been spinning in his head since Friday night, José declarations: Might Makes Right, and the Many Serve the Few.

Jeff began, "We had a great farewell gathering at The Thirsty Scholar while I was working Friday night. Just about every one of my good friends was able to make it. And, as was seeming to be becoming the custom, most stayed until closing. But I wanted to talk to you about one of the conversations we had that night."

Papa's attention grew focused as he could sense the gravity in Jeff's voice. "What was it you were talking about?" he inquired.

"The conversation," Jeff explained, "had turned to student debt and the challenging situation most of my friends are finding themselves in. Most are going to be starting their careers already in the hole for tens of thousands of dollars."

"Well, a good college education can be expensive," Papa offered.

"It's more than that," Jeff continued. "It's almost like young people are being set up – forced into a box and shackled with a ball and chain."

Papa noted the seriousness of Jeff's concern. He listened closely.

"José was talking about his going into politics," said Jeff. This was a subject Jeff, Papa, and José had discussed a number of times, even in these very chairs. "José talked about making his fortune in politics, and when Reese and Jennifer challenged him, he raised the specter of two dictates: Might Makes Right, and the Many Serve the Few."

"Elaborate on that a little more," Papa responded. "What did he mean? Or rather, what was the context for making those assertions?"

"Well, you know José. He's always been ambitious, and he's always intended to make it big. But when he made those statements, Might Makes Right and the Many Serve the Few, something clicked – in a bad way – in my head.

"José was talking about the ends justifying the means to make money, in the way politicians make their fortunes. He suggested doing what's right doesn't matter. He summarized the world as shaped and dominated by power. And the masses don't have any power. That seemed to me to be both obvious and appalling."

"Why do you say, 'appalling?'" Papa urged Jeff to dig a little deeper as he sipped his cabernet.

"Because people have been struggling for hundreds of years," said Jeff, "in this country and around the world, for freedom and equality. What José suggested made it painfully obvious to me that that struggle may still even be in vain.

"While we may progress two steps forward, we continue to take one step back, and sometimes more than one step. Very few seem to be enjoying the benefits of the advances we make. The system ensures a select few get what they want, when they want it. And we, the masses, continue to struggle."

Papa put down his wine glass and shifted in his rocker. He signaled Jeff to put another log on the fire. He then sighed a deep sigh. Jeff had struck a nerve.

"I think it's time to tell you a story my father told me a long, long time ago," Papa said.

Jeff noticed Papa's tone turn solemn; maybe a better way to describe it was melancholy. He had heard this tone only on rare occasions. Jeff realized in an instant this was going to be special.

"I've told you," continued Papa, "Louis – my father and your grandfather – was a language teacher back in France when I was a boy. You know all those details. And I've also told you that my father helped out in the community in a variety of ways. One of those contributions he made was tending sheep when needed, and I helped out on occasion."

"I remember," said Jeff, "you pointed out the hillsides and pastures where your community flocks used to graze. You showed me when we all visited a couple of years ago."

Papa made an effort to travel back to France every few years to visit relatives. That time Lizzie, Jeff, and Jess had accompanied him. Most of Papa's generation of family had passed, but he still kept in touch with what had been childhood friends and extended family members.

"I remember it was the month of May," Jeff continued. Papa could not bring himself to spring for the "high-season" ticket prices of summer, so fall and spring were the usual options. "And the weather was miserable there in Normandy."

"Yes, the weather is often miserable in May." Papa looked deep into the fire, as if traveling back in time. "And it just so happened to be a damp May evening when my father told me this tale." Papa turned back to Jeff and looked him squarely in the eyes. Jeff knew whatever Papa was about to say was important.

"My father and I were tending sheep one evening in the Normandy hills not far from Bayeux. We were huddled under a shelter sharing some bread and cheese. Rain was falling, the air was cold, and the wind was biting. The sheep weren't enjoying the weather any more than we were. They had pretty much settled down for the evening.

"I was eight years old. We had been through a lot. The year was 1944. The Nazis were occupying France. My family and our community had endured grave pain and great loss. Times were hard. And though I really didn't understand how bad things were, I knew that since we had lost Elise a shadow had been hanging over the family."

Papa told a good story. Jeff's attention was transfixed. Even Madeleine listened intently.

Papa carried on, "But even as bad as things were for my family, we were not the worst off in the community. Not at all. So my parents kept up a good front and tried to help

68

those less fortunate, wherever and whenever they could. Our lives were tough; times were tough. I knew my father was hurting." Papa waved his hand toward the fire and continued. "But I could also sense an ember of hope still burning, a spark of hope alive deep within him. He always tried to be positive and optimistic about our situation, particularly with me. I didn't know the whole world was burning, but I had this foreboding sense that our piece of it wasn't right.

"I didn't know exactly what I was saying, but I had to ask." Papa sipped his wine. "I asked my father, 'Is life always going to be like this?'"

Papa paused. He reflected for a moment silently; he was there in those fields on a cold, damp night. He continued, "My father didn't know what to make of the question I was asking, so he inquired, 'What do you mean?'

"I went on to explain about the German soldiers pushing people around, even beating and killing some. The curfews, the pulled window shades, and quiet whisperings. This was all I knew, but not what I was taught life could be. I asked my father, 'Why is there so much fear?'"

Papa rocked gently back in his chair as he repeated, slowly and painfully, "Why is there so much fear?"

"My father understood the anxiety I felt. He was trying to teach me that these were not normal times and that life could be better than this. But I didn't know any other way. So I was asking him, 'Why is life this way?'

"Papa looked at me and said, 'Nicolas...'" Papa's name was Nicolas. Papa's father, Louis, a student of linguistics, chose Nicolas as the name for his first child, his son, as Nicolas was a derivative of the Greek Nikolaos, meaning "victory of the people."

Nicolas was born in 1936 as a dark cloud was rising on the continent. A specter of fear was growing, consuming all in its path. Life was being made increasingly difficult and dangerous by the choices of men. Louis had heard the warnings of his brother Marcel and others and recognized the danger. The name Nicolas was a reminder and a hope: a reminder that the people possess the power; and a hope that the people would exercise that power to restore peace – victory of the people.

Papa continued, "My father said, 'Nicolas, I need to tell you a story. It's a story of creation. An aspect of the creation story you are not familiar with; a detail about creation I think it's time I shared.'"

Papa reached for his wine glass again and Jeff followed suit.

Then Papa explained, "My father told me this myth while we were tending sheep in the fields of Normandy. Less than a month later, my father was killed helping the Allies during the D-Day invasion there in Normandy. This is the tale I need to tell you now.

"To begin with, God created the earth in seven days. Isn't that right, Jefferson?" Papa inquired whimsically, using his hands to make the story come alive.

"That's right," Jeff responded. "Or so it is written in the Book of Genesis."

Papa continued, "Peter wrote, 'In the Lord's eyes, one day is as a thousand years, and a thousand years are as a day.' He could have as easily said a million years. God is outside time. God can do wondrous things."

Jeff settled in to listen intently. Madeleine closed her eyes, enjoying the heat of the crackling fire and hushed of tones of intimate conversation.

The Story of the Sheep, Herders, and Wolves

God intended to produce a magnificent creation: a dynamic, growing, evolving, loving, living creation.

He established time as a way to observe and experience His wonderful, awesome creation as it transformed, developed, and progressed. He fixed time to move in one direction, but since His system, His creation was not static; to ensure the system did not rush to either consolidate or disintegrate, He made the universe and all its component parts operate in cycles.

His design ebbed and flowed, expanded and contracted, grew and evolved; elements aged, died, decayed, and were ever renewed and born again. It was a magnificent creation.

On the first day God said, "Let there be light," and there was light. God separated the light from the darkness, and He set in place the sun and moon.

On the third day God made this world come alive. His creation moved and changed. This living system, flourishing by means of cycles, tipped one way and then the other, always settling back to balance. This was a splendid creation.

Then on the sixth day God created all kinds of living creatures – cattle, creeping things, and wild animals.

Well, there is more to that sixth day than the passages of Genesis convey.

God ignited His creation – the universe – as an expanse; an expansion.

The greatest force in existence is God; and God is love.

Love is a force that drives all to cooperate and collaborate, to sacrifice, give and forgive, to ultimately unite, come together and achieve perfection – to reunite in God, as God: to become whole.

Love animates the universe. Love draws all things together. Nothing is as powerful or as awesome as love. God imbued life itself with the force of love – a dynamic striving to grow and evolve together in harmony.

God created sentient beings as a way to explore and experience His creation in time and space.

To feel and embrace the ultimate experience – the joy of unbounded, absolute, infinite, unconditional love – sentient creatures had to experience contrast. Immersed in love, we'd know nothing else; but to come to embrace love and feel its ultimate joy and majesty we must experience what is other than love.

God established a balance within creation: darkness to light, growth to decline, birth to death, suffering to exaltations, pain to joy. By experiencing that which is other than love, we come to recognize, appreciate, and ultimately embrace love. Love is the one constant, the one unconditional, steadfast, and enduring element of God's creation.

Upon all the animals and insects, birds and fish and reptiles, everything He made to explore His creation, God bestowed the power of will; that is, motivation to move and act, and instincts to guide actions.

God instilled in all creatures two dominant traits to help ensure their survival. The first was an all-powerful motivating force – fear. Wherever fear dominates, might would triumph – might makes right.

The second was an energy conservation device. As survival depended on a creature's ability to secure and maintain energy – food – conserving energy, doing only the minimum necessary, allowed a creature to survive longer. To survive, God's creatures try to get the most with the least effort.

But God intended for life to do more than just survive, He intended for life to grow and flourish. To that end He determined to fashion beings that could do more than just maintain the system. God intended on forming beings that could actually *create*.

God wanted to craft a being which had aspects of His divinity; which had consciousness; the ability to travel

74

through time, and the ability to create seemingly from nothing.

God had a vision for humanity.

Human beings would have the ability to see themselves in relation to other beings. They could anticipate a future and draw from learning in the past in ways other creatures could not.

He planned to create sentient beings with a purpose to explore and experience His magnificent creation; with the ability to learn and grow; and with the ultimate gift to create and contribute. Through these gifts humans could come to embrace and embody love.

Mankind would be His vehicle for extraordinary evolution.

But before creating humans, God had work to do.

God realized that if He endowed creatures with a uniquely dominant trait, those creatures generally relied on that trait to survive.

If He endowed an animal with great size or strength or speed, that animal leveraged that attribute but rarely capitalized on other qualities. In a physical world, size, strength, and speed matter; the biggest, strongest, fastest and most ruthless dominate. Might makes right.

However, endowing a creature with great intelligence, giving them the ability to figure out in a broad sense how things worked and how the environment and other animals behaved, was potentially an even more powerful asset. Creatures with intelligence and cunning stood out. Even when competing against larger, stronger, and faster adversaries, intelligent and cunning creatures could survive and thrive.

Even so, God was imagining something grander still.

If He did not give a creature commanding physical attributes such as size, strength, speed, or another trait to conquer the environment and other creatures, then in order to survive, that creature would, of necessity, be forced to cooperate and collaborate with others of its kind. By collaborating they could leverage the attributes and the inherent strength of the community. Those beings, by coming together, would begin to discover the power of unity, of love – that all-powerful force of creation.

God had a vision of greatness evolving from humble beginnings.

A being set free on earth could evolve and create in concert with, and caring for all, of the earth's systems. This being could ultimately flourish and expand out into, and then

76

beyond, physical limitations. God's creation could explore and experience all dimensions of His universe.

This was the making of a glorious adventure.

God sought to determine just what attributes would serve His ultimate vision.

Before He fashioned the first human, before He blew into his nostrils the breath of life; God conducted an experiment.

He surveyed His creation and focused His gaze on a humble creature.

Sheep were wonderful animals. They were docile and friendly, social and loving, hardy and resilient. They cared

for their young. They cared for each other, and not having dominant physical attributes in a competitive world, sheep worked together to ensure all lived in safety.

God looked lovingly on his sheep. Sheep would test His theory.

In a world of bigger, faster, stronger, more dangerous and more aggressive creatures, sheep needed a competitive edge. Uniting and working together was that competitive edge.

Sheep were social creatures that responded to social cues. Individual sheep did whatever the sheep around them did. They followed the herd, for better or for worse.

The sheep's ability to prosper was limited by fear and a need to conserve energy.

To pull the sheep together and get them to work together and move in safe, productive, and fruitful directions, God realized the sheep needed leadership. The sheep needed strong and noble leaders: guides, guardians, shepherds – herders.

Leaders are first and foremost servants. Leaders – good leaders, noble, principled, self-less leaders — are the few serving the many. Working together under the direction, guidance, and tutelage of selfless herders, simple, humble sheep were a powerful force.

To begin His experiment, God endowed sheep with a transformative ability.

Each and every sheep could continue his or her life as a sheep. Striving to live a comfortable and safe life, all a sheep had to do was conform and contribute as directed. They only had to follow the flock, blend in with the herd, and do the minimum required. Not much would be asked of them and not much would be demanded.

To survive – and following the right path, to thrive – each sheep would have to merely contribute the necessary effort to remain adequately comfortable and reasonably safe. In a highly competitive world, some sheep would be lost, but most, if they conformed and gave their fair share responding to good leadership, would thrive.

God, however, gave the sheep two other choices.

The first choice was
that every individual
sheep had the ability – of
his or her own free will
and choosing – to
transform into a leader: a
sheep herder.

Each sheep could choose to remain a sheep and do as he
or she was guided and instructed; or that sheep could
determine to assume the mantle of leadership; of herder.

Herders received the gifts of size and strength, speed and
vision. Herders were mighty. Herders applied their might to
care for the sheep and guide the flock.

It was a herder's job to lead the sheep to fruitful pastures.
It was a herder's job to ensure the sheep did not over
consume and overwhelm the environment. It was a herder's
job to prepare the sheep for difficult times and lead them
through challenging circumstances. It was a herder's job to
protect the flock from everything that might threaten the
sheep: predators, the environment, or even disharmony
amongst members of the herd.

More was asked of and demanded of herders.

Herders saw from a broader perspective and developed characteristics sheep didn't need. To be a herder required discipline and sacrifice and effort – hard work. Herders drew from a wellspring of energy and insight common sheep would not expend the effort to hone and sharpen. Herders were guided by overarching principles of service and sacrifice; selfless values necessary to ensure the flock flourished.

Herders led the flock, guarded the flock, and protected the flock. Herders would, if necessary, lay down their lives for the sheep. Good herders were admired and beloved by the sheep.

With honest, brave, caring, and insightful herders, the sheep thrived and prospered. The sheep evolved and grew plentiful.

While the collective herd of sheep always maintained the power, individual sheep chose what they independently wanted to be. Most chose the relative ease and comfort of being sheep. Only a select few took on the mantle of leadership. With enough sheep making the right choice, all the sheep profited and lived full and fulfilling lives.

Under the right leadership of principled, selfless, and wise herders, the sheep could come to dominate the earth.

But having only one direction to go was not God's plan. He sought more.

God intended to endow the pinnacle of creation with free will – the ability to choose any path. Having free will, God's creatures could choose either a good path or a bad path. God gave the sheep a second choice.

This reality of time and space was a place to experience contrast. Having free will meant all aspects of contrast were in play and were options for God's creation.

The first choice was that each sheep, of his or her own free will and choosing, could decide to transform into a herder. The second choice was to choose to transform into a wolf.

Like herders, wolves were large and strong, fast and

cunning. They possessed dangerous weapons: piercing claws, powerful jaws, and razor-sharp fangs.

As predators, not protectors, wolves were feared by the flock. Wolves killed with impunity. Wolves took what they wanted, when they wanted. Wolves looked out solely for themselves. The power and freedom of being a wolf was tempting, tantalizing, and alluring to many sheep.

Wolves were the pariahs of the flock. The only thing standing in the way of wolves decimating the flock were herders – guardians of the sheep.

Each sheep could remain a sheep for a portion of, or for all, of their lives. They could seek comfort and safety, contribute the minimum necessary, and conform to whatever the flock demanded.

Life would be simple.

With the right leadership; with a few good herders serving the many, life would at least be, if not easy, manageable. Sheep would not expect too much, nor would too much be demanded of them.

They would live, explore and experience, learn and grow, create and contribute within the confines of the flock. Nothing too extraordinary, nothing too audacious; but nothing too overwhelming or too threatening either.

Life would be simple, and hopefully safe and serene.

The sheep would neither venture much nor risk much; they would have to put forth effort for themselves and the community, but never too much. Life would come and life would go, and the flock would carry on.

To choose to become a herder was a risky option.

Herders developed size and strength and speed, and being a herder meant acquiring status – the sheep looked up to and relied upon their herders. But being a herder meant study and learning, diligence and discipline, risk and threat and danger. The rewards of being a herder were remarkable, extraordinary, but also taxing and troubling and effortful. Being a herder was hard and noble work.

Few answered the call.

Choosing to become a wolf, on the other hand, was liberating on many levels.

Like herders, wolves had extraordinary assets, including size, strength, and  speed. Wolves were smart and cunning and dangerous. Wolves were mighty. However, wolves were not guided by

84

selfless principles. Wolves were free to do as they pleased. They did not answer to anyone or anything. They did not feel responsible to anyone or anything. They did not have to conform or comply or contribute. Wolves lived for themselves and used their might for themselves.

God set His experiment in motion and watched as flocks of sheep evolved.

Life for a small flock of sheep was challenging. Herders always emerged from small flocks. Herders were necessary for small flocks to survive the elements and predators.

But curious developments always arose as flocks matured in size and power. As the size of a flock grew, a few sheep always chose to be wolves. Some sheep just didn't like putting forth effort for the benefit of others. Or they didn't like the conformity of the flock. They wanted power and status, but they didn't want to work hard or take on a mantle of leadership with its inherent responsibility. These sheep preferred to take, not give.

Sheep choosing to be wolves wanted *freedom and power without responsibility*.

Wolves would seek out, attack, and kill the weakest and most vulnerable of the flock. Herders tirelessly defended the sheep from any and every attack. Good herders eliminated

85

threats and made the wolves' lives difficult; much harder, in fact, than sheep had imagined or hoped for before they became wolves. Good herders working together were always a step or two ahead of the wolves.

But as you might imagine, times changed.

When flocks were small and threats were menacing, fear motivated the sheep. Being able to overcome fear, sheep banded together and leaders emerged. The sheep followed those leaders.

As herders proved effective, times became prosperous, and life for the sheep was less dangerous and taxing, the size and strength of the herd grew. As threats subsided and life became easy, fear diminished as a motivator, and increasingly sheep grew complacent, lazy, and bored. An easy comfortable life bred jealousy, envy, and mischief.

When times were too good, too stress-free, and too comfortable, some sheep looked to achieve status an easy way. These sheep chose to become wolves. They determined, "Why work for others or the community, or put in the effort needed to be a herder, when you could break out on your own and become a wolf?"

Built into the good times and the sheep's nature was a means to undermine community, destabilize stability, and

86

impoverish prosperity. It all came down to a choice and an individual decision.

Free will gave the sheep the options of choosing a stable way (stay as sheep and contribute), a challenging way (develop into a herder and lead), or the option of choosing power and status without responsibility, a vision of the ultimate easy, well-to-do life (become a wolf). What every sheep aspired to when good times abounded.

Freedom without responsibility is always an attractive choice. We aspire to power and status without effort or obligation. We believe "getting" or "taking" is more fruitful and more enriching than is "giving."

It's all an illusion. It's a deception and a delusion.

87

There is no such thing as freedom without responsibility. Thinking this aberration is possible – having freedom without responsibility – is a trap into which far too many willingly succumb.

In the ability to unite and create, God saw in His creations an opportunity for greatness; and in the ability to choose apparently easy and rewarding, but ultimately painful and destructive paths, He saw an opportunity for calamity.

He endowed His creation with free will. And the drama unfolded.

God watched a social cycle develop. Challenges, of necessity, produced leaders – selfless, principled, honest, caring leaders. Sheep became herders to guide and protect the flock. The few served the many.

When during times of plenty the multitude of sheep had everything they needed, they tended to ignore herders.

For varied reasons, some sheep – seeking status, power or perceived freedom – always chose the ostensibly easy, high-status path. They chose to be wolves. Wolves attempted to misdirect, divide, and kill the sheep. But herders continually stood ready to respond.

Whenever the flock was threatened, by the environment, by wolves and other predators, or by disharmony amongst sheep, the sheep rallied and leaders emerged. Sheep selflessly stepped forward to assume the mantle of leadership to guide and empower the flock. The power always remained with the community – the sheep individually and the flock collectively always possessed the ultimate power.

How that power was used came down to individual choices made by sheep.

Good times never lasted however, because as life for the sheep got easier and the motivation of fear subsided, the sheep focused less on the community and more on themselves. When things became too good and too easy, more sheep, lured by the promises of status and power and independence, would choose to become wolves. The sheep that became wolves saw they could have more while doing less than sheep working within the flock. They saw a route to more comfort and less commitment – always an attractive alternative when the risks seemed small.

The cycle progressed.

As wolves grew in number, they became more brazen and bold. Initially they applied aggressive tactics to plunder sheep, but herders proved to be worthy adversaries. To avoid confronting herders directly, wolves turned to more devious and sophisticated tactics.

Wolves began to disguise themselves.

They interacted
with the sheep
planting seeds of
distrust and division.
They undermined
genuine selfless
leaders.

Ingeniously disguised as sheep or even as herders, wolves promised sheep ever greater ease and comfort if only they would do as the wolves directed. They promised the sheep everything from ease and comfort to status and power.

Many of the sheep, seeking the easiest path, were misled by false promises, and the wolves would strike.

It wasn't that the sheep were stupid; it was that the sheep – being sheep – always sought the path of least resistance and the easy alternative. They were easily manipulated by fear and the tantalizing offer of ease and comfort.

The wolves' most powerful tactics included pointing to a seemingly easy way or dividing the sheep and threatening them, stoking fear. Sheep successfully segregated by wolves were fearful. Sheep divided were weak. But even those sheep still united in a flock fell for the lie, again and again. That lie was: *They could get something for nothing.*

Only when all easy and supposedly free alternatives were exhausted would sheep put forth the effort necessary to advance. When the flock pulled together, the sheep learned they all – each and every one – had to contribute for the group to succeed.

But when green pastures were bountiful, the weather comfortable, and threats subsided, community invariably broke down. "Pulling together" increasing turned into "every sheep for himself." It was then when more and more sheep chose to become wolves.

Over time, as the struggle for the soul of the flock grew, more sheep were killed and more joined the ranks of the wolves.

As the sentiment of the flock turned toward the wolves, even herders grew weary. Tired of trying to guide sheep that resisted the better options requiring work and effort, herders were enticed by the allure of wolves. Herders who transformed to wolves became the most powerful of predators, as they had secured the trust of the sheep.

As the power of wolves grew, the cycle progressed to chaos.

Might alone ruled. Might made right.

Wolves isolated the sheep and divided the flock. They found the "every sheep for himself" culture was ideal for segregating individual sheep and usurping the sheep's power. Wolves attacked and killed sheep indiscriminately.

Eventually, the wolves dominated and enslaved the sheep.

The many came to serve the few.

As wolves ascended to power, fewer and fewer herders were likely to arise. Without the support of the flock,

92

genuine caring, committed, competent, and courageous leaders – herders – were no match for swarming packs of wolves.

God watched as flock after flock went through this cycle. But He knew what came next.

Wolves by their nature – being self-seeking and self-absorbed – always nurtured their own undoing. One of two things repeatedly happened.

In some flocks, as wolves began to multiply, the sheep would unite, new leaders would emerge, and together the herd would fend off and ultimately defeat the wolves. These flocks grew in size and strength and prospered.

In other flocks however, if the wolves were able to dominate the herders and the flock, the wolves plundered and decimated the sheep. Fearful sheep scattered and hid, attempting to survive, thereby further isolating the remaining sheep.

As sheep grew scarce, the wolves turned on each other. They fought amongst themselves until nearly nothing was left. The wolves, selfish and self-seeking, always proved to be their own worst enemies.

A healthy flock, recognizing the false promises of charlatan wolves, would unite to overcome the internal threat before it undermined the community. Small flocks, threatened by the environment and predators, including wolves arising from their own ranks, learned to rely on noble, selfless leaders to survive and ultimately thrive.

Some sheep always chose to be wolves, but they were a nuisance a healthy flock could easily overcome. If the sheep came together, leaders would arise and the flock would advance.

The challenge to the flock, however, always arose when times were good, when sheep had plenty and felt safe and secure. Prosperity and the power of  community often led to complacency and envy. Complacency and envy gave birth to a new effort: causing sheep to choose the path of wolf. By means of cunning and deceit, wolves commandeered the power of the herd.

In unhealthy flocks, sheep dispersed and hid. Some sheep simply chose to become wolves. The wolves first enslaved

94

and then massacred the flock. The sheep were sheared and then they were skewered.

The Many Served the Few

After destroying what sustained their existence, the wolves turned on each other. Surviving sheep would begin anew. The cycled played out over and over again.

God allowed sheep to make their choice. The power always rested with the sheep.

They could choose to explore and experience, learn and grow, create and contribute uniting in love, and to become whole and expand in community with other sheep. Or they could choose to secure power and status for themselves, and the whole effort, the entire adventure, would culminate in hatred, conflict, and ultimately violence.

Freedom, opportunity and risk: God saw what he had created was good.

By giving the ultimate power to the sheep, each sheep could choose his or her own path, for better or for worse. Each sheep could choose to be a conduit for creativity and inspiration – a vessel for love. Or each sheep could choose a different path – one of corruption and chaos.

God's gifts, the attributes He bestowed, were an opportunity for either unity and prosperity or division and destruction.

Freedom always offers multiple options. God determined to grant these gifts He had given these sheep to an even more advanced and capable being.

And here we are.

"This cycle of challenge, growth, and prosperity nurturing the seeds of chaos and destruction is a cycle we are entrusted to break," said Papa as the embers glowed red in the fireplace. "My father told me the wolves had arisen there in Europe while the sheep stood by. But finally in those dark, dismal days, the sheep had finally chosen to unite and fend off the wolves. My father assured me that soon, times would be different. Life would get better, for us and for everyone.

""Nicolas,' my father implored me those many years ago, 'Watch out! This cycle is a part of human nature. It will play out again. When it seems as though it is every man for himself, beware the wolves. It will be your turn to choose, your time to choose. It will be up to the people to choose. Will you stand together or fall apart?'"

- 4 -

VICTORY OF THE PEOPLE

Papa looked at Jeff with hope in his eyes. "You see, Jefferson, God always leaves the choice to us. If everyone does his or her part, we can live a pretty good life. We can blend into the crowd, as most of us do most of the time. We can enjoy the love of friends and family and of community. Not a bad life. Do what we must, contribute where we can, and we all get by.

"Or we can take on more than the average person and choose to lead. We can guide people to overcome whatever might inhibit personal growth, and by doing so, strengthen our community. If we're lucky, we can do what good leaders are meant to do: unite people, inspire prosperity, and advance our progression into love."

Then Papa slowly shook his head. "We are also free to choose a darker path."

Madeleine opened her eyes, stood up, arched her back in a long deep stretch, then circled around on her pillow and settled back down. She knew the conversation was far from over.

Papa, too, needed to stretch his legs, and also refill his wine. With effort and a bit of a muffled groan he rocked forward and lifted himself from his chair. "What say you, young Jefferson?"

"You mean about the story you just told?"

Papa smiled and raised his glass, "No – I mean, do you want me to top off your glass?"

"Thanks, Papa." Jeff held out his wine glass for Papa to pour.

Jeff then placed another log on the fire.

The cribbage match had stalled as Papa spun his tale. But move forward it must. Papa sat back down and dealt the next hand of cards. The play continued.

"So Papa," Jeff asked, "you think we're parading through this cycle once again?"

Papa reflected for a few seconds. "Jefferson, I read a book a number of years ago which was published a few years before you were born. The book was written by a couple of think-tank guys from DC. The title of the book was *The Fourth Turning*. In that book the authors outlined a theory about social cycles.

98

"The authors had this idea that just like natural cycles of, let's say, the planets in orbit, the turning of the seasons, or the phases of an animal's life, we are immersed in *social cycles*. These cycles are bigger than individuals or communities or even nations. We are all affected by these cycles.

"Good times, when people are pulling together, are followed by a slow unsettling and division. Eventually the predominant attitude becomes 'every man for himself.' The conclusion of a full turn of a cycle is a decision point, where there is both a crisis and an opportunity."

Papa poked the air with his finger for emphasis. "The cycle culminates in chaos, where the people are left to choose to unite or divide, pull together or fall apart. Which option we choose determines our fate. I think we are approaching that decision point again."

A calamity is in the offing, Jeff thought to himself, and we're here sipping wine and playing cards.

Papa recognized the look of concern on Jeff's face. He swallowed some more fine cabernet. "*The Fourth Turning* explained in contemporary detail the truth my father had expressed to me back in May of 1944."

The card play continued as their discussion evolved. Jeff tallied his hand and advanced his pegs along the board. Papa counted the points in his hand and then in the crib and advanced his peg as well. Papa then shuffled the deck for the next deal.

The game of cribbage was familiar and comforting, but the ideas the two were discussing made Jeff increasingly uncomfortable. He raised a point of concern. "A cycle that is beyond our ability to influence doesn't seem much like freedom or free will. Are we fated or perhaps doomed to follow a prescribed path?"

"I don't think so," Papa replied. "God's creation, by design, demands we move. We are on an adventure through time and space. Our purpose is to explore and experience, learn and grow, create and contribute, as we return to God."

Papa had spent a lifetime considering these notions. "God experiences His creation through us. We are meant to have, or at least are given, the greatest of opportunities: to reunite in love with God." Papa smiled.

The two had discussed this "purpose of life" many times, but Papa now offered a new perspective. "I've been thinking about humanity's resistance to spiritual evolution. We keep digging the same holes, making the same mistakes, fighting

100

the same petty battles." Papa had been struggling with these concepts quite a bit lately. Jeff realized Papa was breaking new ground.

Papa continued, "It seems people mature through this purpose of exploring and experiencing, learning and growing, and finally creating and contributing. Unfortunately, many of us just don't want to advance."

"What do you mean, Papa?" Jeff inquired.

"God gave us a creation with two constants: change – which is this creation – and His guiding love. He gave us a creation to experience and His love to guide us through that creation. That everything is in motion and constantly changing, we automatically and by design must move and explore. We take in or feel or experience all we encounter."

"And God guides our advance," Jeff affirmed.

Papa appreciated that Jeff agreed and added, "We have embedded in our beings this capacity and this propensity to learn and grow. Our bodies change, our desires change, and our perspectives change quite naturally and somewhat automatically. The challenge is that people have the ability to resist even what God set us in motion to do."

"We have the free will to resist," Jeff rephrased.

Nodding agreement, Papa resumed, "Many stop exploring. And many stop experiencing. We resist change. We find a comfortable position, or at least what we think is a manageable position, then we cling tightly to what we have and what we know. We stop moving forward. And we stop learning and growing – unfortunately, too often at the earliest opportunity."

"Why do you think we do that, Papa?"

Papa had taught Jeff to never assume it's "they" who have it wrong, or "they, them, those others" who make mistakes. Papa constantly reminded Jeff that the two of them were not perfect, the two of them also made mistakes, the two of them often chose the easy path over the right path, and the two of them were as culpable as everyone else. Papa encouraged Jeff from an early age to recognize that he, like all people, had a responsibility to, and a share in, society. Whatever the circumstances, good or bad, it's never "their fault"; it's always "our fault." Papa explained that by taking responsibility, you always ensure you hold onto your power.

Papa went on, "We determine that constantly exploring and experiencing and endlessly learning and growing requires too much effort. Remember the sheep; they prefer the easy way."

"Path of least resistance creatures; that we are," Jeff reaffirmed.

Papa summarized, "We think it's easier to define a position, build a shell, and then do what we can to defend that position. We human beings hate change."

Change, and particularly this idea of our resistance to change, was a topic Jeff and Papa had discussed many times.

"What about the creating and contributing part?" Jeff probed.

"Many of us never mature enough to embrace that aspect of our nature and our purpose," replied Papa. "For an individual to realize their potential, he or she must express the gifts God has given them. We are each meant to share our talents and to contribute in community."

Jeff finished the thought: "And we each have the gift to create, which in and of itself is a collective enterprise."

"Too many of us never come to realize why we are here," Papa continued. "We stop exploring and experiencing, and cling to what we believe is 'good enough.' We stop learning and growing, as letting go and learning is just way too hard. So we never come to realize the majesty of God's greatest gift – the power to create and contribute, and to give.

When one of us stops advancing toward his or her potential, we all pay the price."

Jeff, having listened closely, and knowing Papa's optimistic disposition, interjected, "But you said the two constants in life were change and God's guiding love."

"That's right, Jefferson! Despite our hard-headedness," Papa paused for a moment, "and our hard-*heartedness*, God is constantly imploring us, guiding us, and asking us to follow a better path."

"So there is always hope?"

"There is always hope, my good man. There is always hope," Papa smiled. After pausing to lay down two cards for the crib, Papa began again. "God established life would unfold in cycles. Think of a cycle this way, Jefferson. Imagine we are on an amusement park ride; perhaps a roller coaster. Remember the first time I took you on a roller coaster at Cedar Point?"

"Yes, I do," Jeff smiled incredulously. "I lost my lunch."

"Well, at least we were off the coaster when that happened."

"That's true." Jeff nodded his head.

"A car on a roller coaster has to climb a hill to store up potential energy," continued Papa. "It releases that energy as

104

it coasts down. Then it begins to climb again. Through cycles, God ensures a means of coming back into balance."

Jeff was following Papa's line of thinking and summarized his point. "We have an opportunity to experience extremes, and when we stray from the best path and ignore God's guidance, because life operates in cycles, we are always offered a way back to balance, a way back on to a better path."

"I think so." Papa then let out a satisfied sigh.

Jeff, a little suspicious, wasn't sure if Papa was reaffirming this train of thought, or whether he was holding a great cribbage hand.

Papa looked Jeff straight in the eyes and said, "We can progress forward as long as we work together – as long as we collaborate and cooperate."

Jeff filled in the alternative: "Or we can fall apart, go out on our own, with every man for himself, and endure the pain of that choice. I saw the positive example of this at the Wexler's anniversary party last night. And I heard the negative from Father Joseph telling us about the Bosnian wars this morning."

"Indeed," Papa agreed. "If we do stray, life always presents a means to move back into balance. God never leaves us alone. He is always calling us to goodness. He is always calling us home."

Then Jeff asserted, "But we don't have to go."

Papa drew a deep breath. "That's right. It seems, however, the consequences of making a wrong turn and then not choosing to move back into balance can be quite dire."

Heady talk about weighty subjects.

Jeff was inching ahead on the cribbage board. But Papa kept him in his sights. Sometimes it was not a player's game play, tactics, or strategy that determined the outcome, but the cards.

"In your telling of that creation story," said Jeff, "you kept emphasizing this notion that the people – or rather, the sheep – possess the power. Looking at us human beings, how can that be so? The people, the masses, seem to have very little power."

"Do you really think so, Jefferson?" Papa questioned. "Is it that the people don't have power, or that they willingly give up or forfeit their power, and they choose not to exercise it?" Papa decided to apply a tactic he learned from those brief years spent with his father. "Let's start with the basics, the fundamentals; shall we?"

"I thought you might say that," Jeff said with sincerity. On countless occasions across a wide range of topics, Papa had used the "fundamentals" approach to school Jeff.

Gleaning consent, Papa queried, "What is fundamental to human nature, Jefferson?"

This was ground Jeff had tread with Papa many times before. Jeff responded, "On the most fundamental level people, are seeking to survive."

"Yes, that's a base instinct. We want to survive. So what motivates us, what drives us, what allows us to survive?" Papa began peeling back the onion.

"Well, first of all, having limited strength and speed, we must rely on one another to live. There is no such thing as going it alone. By design and by necessity, we must care for and look out for one another."

"So we are social creatures?" Papa probed.

"Yes," Jeff confirmed.

"So," Papa continued, not missing a beat, "not being the biggest, the strongest, the fastest, nor perhaps even the brightest, in this competitive world characterized by an unforgiving environment and populated by myriad threats, to survive we must rely on community?"

"Most certainly," Jeff asserted. "We're in this together. All of us. An individual would not, could not, survive on his or her own. We are social creatures who must collaborate and cooperate to survive. And more than that, we must collaborate and cooperate to thrive and prosper."

Papa laid down a card to total fifteen, and then asked, "But what about the individual? What drives an individual?"

They were rehashing familiar themes, but by reviewing they often arrived at new destinations. This is why Jeff loved these conversations. He answered, "Well, like Maslow theorized, individuals first seek to fulfill their immediate physical needs and to ensure safety. Then they seek to belong."

"And what comes after belonging?" asked Papa.

Jeff knew immediately: "Esteem."

"Status! Now there's an interesting observation." Papa implied they were getting somewhere. He then circled back. "Realizing all of that – Maslow's theory of hierarchy of needs – what do you think are people's most powerful drives?"

"Well, people will do anything, and sometimes *must* do anything, for food and water – the essentials needed to survive," Jeff responded.

"But is there something which will influence even the need for food and water? Something that harkens back predominantly to the need to survive?" Papa was getting to the root of his inquiry.

"Are you talking about fear?"

"Yes! Precisely! *Fear!*" They had arrived. Papa persisted, "Fear is a base motivation. Fear, fear of loss – of something, anything – is the great motivator. Of course, fear has a practical purpose. It keeps us from doing risky or dangerous things. Fear keeps us from forfeiting our lives. But fear is a trait, a characteristic, an instinct which can also be leveraged against us."

Papa stressed his point, "Since fear is a common, base motivation, we have come to employ it – fear – as the predominant means to manipulate one another. Fear is an inherent quality that acts to counter absolute freedom, and, you could say, free will. Fear keeps us from doing any and everything we want."

Papa had now established a foundation from which to expand the conversation. "Fear is a base motivation. But let's turn to the other side of the equation. What is it people desire most?"

"They just want to be happy," Jeff responded.

"What does that mean?" pressed Papa.

"They simply want to feel good."

"I think you are on to something, Jefferson." Papa laid down his last card. They each in turn tallied up their hands and then Papa tallied the crib. Papa was closing the gap Jeff had worked so hard to establish in this second game.

"People certainly want to feel good," said Papa, picking up the theme. "Moment to moment, people always seek to feel better." He looked at Jeff. Madeleine began to stir. She slowly rose to her feet; stretched, then made her way to her water bowl in the kitchen. She was illustrating Papa's point.

"People certainly want to be happy," Papa continued. "But happiness for most translates into feeling good in the moment: a full belly, comfortable temperatures, a safe environment. In the moment, when not threatened, we spend most of our time, energy, and effort changing how we feel. We are always seeking to feel better. And if we have a full belly, we want to be entertained."

"Ah, *panem et cirsenses*." Jeff knew where Papa was going, referring to the Roman political strategy of appeasing the masses with bread and games. Jeff harmonized further, "Unfortunately, most of us never anticipate the future consequences of immediate gratification."

110

"That's right, Jefferson! We want to feel good right now, with a full belly and engaging entertainment." Papa intended to define where the two of them had arrived. "Let's see. We are social creatures driven by two main urges: fear, as a means to survive; and the need or intention to feel better while conserving energy and putting forth as little effort as possible. We seek always, moment to moment, to feel better."

Jeff had just completed dealing. Papa rearranged the cards in his hand.

"Fear and feeling," Jeff echoed. "It all seems pretty much in the moment. There doesn't seem to be any consideration for the future. But, we can see beyond today."

"Yes, we can. We can see far into the future, Jefferson." Then Papa posed another question. "When considering time – that is, moving beyond the moment – what is it we desire most? What is it *you* might desire most?" Papa wanted to make his question relevant to Jeff and where he was now. "Thinking of your future, Jefferson, what would you most like to have? Let's say, if you found a magic lamp and you were granted one wish; what would you wish for?"

Over the years Papa had proposed just this question to Jeff dozens of times. Each time Jeff answered differently, depending on his circumstances at the moment. He answered "toys" when he was young, and "the attention of a young heartthrob" was once a consideration; but as he got older "money and power" became the dominant themes.

"Well, to tell the truth, I'd ask for the ability to control my life. I'd want to be in control."

"Let's peal that potato a little, shall we," Papa persisted. "When you get down to it, most of us will ask for money and power, or for physical attributes which will ultimately give us the means to acquire influence, leading to money and power – this idea of control, you suggest. We seek power first to ensure we are accepted and belong, and then to acquire esteem or status. Influence, money, and power, for most of us, point to the same thing."

Papa was on a roll. Jeff had brought him precisely to the point he had intended to highlight. "Money, power, and influence are synonymous with control. Whenever we think of anything beyond feeling good in the moment, what we aspire to have most is control."

Jeff clarified and restated, "Once we introduce an element of time – that is, thinking beyond the present moment – what most of us desire is to control what comes next. We all want control over our lives."

112

"I think that's true, Jefferson." Papa then underscored his point. "In the moment, we may be dominated by fear. At those times, dealing with and ridding ourselves of fear is our motivation. If we are free from fear, however, we seek to feel good.

"When we consider a time horizon – beyond the present moment – we seek influence and power. In a word, control. We believe if we can control the circumstances, the conditions, the environment, and most importantly, other people, we can assure ourselves of feeling better."

And Jeff concluded, "And we can ultimately be happy."

"Ah, to be happy!" exclaimed Papa. Then nodding, he summarized, "The three base motivations: fear, feeling, and control. For most of us it all comes down to control. We want it. We believe we need it. We hope and pray and strive to have it."

"But Papa, that's not the way life works."

"Precisely, Jefferson! Quite right! The individual is not in control of the ride. The individual is *on* the ride. So where do we go from here?"

"Well, I think that's game." Jeff enthusiastically laid down his last card, counted up his points, and advanced his peg to win the game. That move meant a third and deciding game was next.

"Well done, Jefferson!" Papa, once again with some effort, got up from his rocking chair. "You tend the fire, set up the board, and shuffle the cards. I'll retrieve the last of our treats."

Papa headed for the refrigerator. Thinking they might get to a third game, he had a dish of select dark chocolates chilling.

For her part, Madeleine had balled up on her bed off the edge of the couch. There she could still sense the warmth of the fire and feel as if she were part of the conversation.

By the time Papa returned to the living room, Jeff had everything set for the third and deciding game. They cut the cards. Jeff held the lower card, which meant the deal was his. He dealt the cards and reached for a chocolate.

"So Papa," he said, "we're fearful sheep, seeking to feel good, but with a drive or desire to attain power."

"Doesn't sound so good when you summarize it like that, Jefferson," Papa said with a twinkle in his eye. "Not exactly how God would want to represent His crowning achievement – a noble, brave, capable, compassionate, selfless, loving creation. But those are our base motivations." Then he

114

circled back to Jeff's concern. "So what about this idea of might makes right?" Papa's style had always been to get Jeff to probe deeper by asking him questions. "When you were a child, you used to complain to me about kids who dominated the playground. What was it about those kids that allowed them to intimidate you?"

"They were the older, bigger, stronger, faster, and more ruthless kids."

"The *mighty*" – Papa stressed that word – "ruled the kingdom."

"Yes, they did." Jeff agreed.

"You see, if we don't mature, if we don't advance and come together – in accordance with God's guidance and our spiritual potential – we rely on our most dominant physical traits."

"As God had foreseen," Jeff asserted.

"We are sheep," Papa continued. "Some of us always turn to the way of the wolf. We leverage strength, speed, and cunning to assert power. The cunning realize that our base desires of fear, fear of loss, and that desire to feel good, in the moment, can be powerful weapons, which can be used to intimidate or manipulate us. By employing fear, and focusing others on feeling good now, wolves rule sheep. And life, to a degree, is *'controlled.'*" Papa feigned quotation marks in the air as he sounded out the word "controlled."

"You see, Jefferson, wolves rule by taking advantage when we're unable or unwilling to exercise our own independent power. We, the sheep, always have the power. We emulate great leaders – herders – when great leaders arise. But we emulate wolves, too, when wolves rise to power."

Jeff, listening carefully, summarized, "In an immature or unhealthy society, individuals leverage might and psychological tactics to intimidate or manipulate sheep in order to, over time, acquire power and gain control."

"We're certainly on the same page, Jefferson." Papa then seized on an opportunity to pivot in a new direction. "You just said 'society,' Jefferson." He paused. "So let's think about this. We're more than individuals – we are community – a society."

"In this together," Jeff pivoted with him. "Right. We've already determined an individual alone cannot survive. The key is the community, the society – how we do what we do *together*."

"So let's think about the community," Papa suggested. And then he continued, "This is where José's assertion, 'The

116

Many Serve the Few,' comes in." He studied his cards. Discarding a pair for the crib, he continued philosophizing. "In our physical world, Jefferson, in our prosperous, consumer-oriented society, what seems to be the most important thing to most people?"

"Well, as we've surmised, on an individual level we seek to be happy."

"Yes, that's true. But on a societal level, in this county, in the United States of Plenty, what do most us believe will make us happy?"

"More stuff."

"And how do we typically get more stuff?"

"With money."

"Exactly, money! Money is our common means to power – to stuff – to control. For us, money translates into power." Papa was satisfied they were making acceptable progress. Glancing at the cribbage board, however, he realized he had to buckle down a little.

"We're right back at that theme of power," he continued. "We all want to be happy. We sheep want good, comfortable, happy lives. But we sheep don't want to put forth too much effort." After discarding his last card four points shy of thirty-one, he then continued, "However, for the flock to survive, leaders – shepherds, herders – are required. A few sheep must rise to lead and serve. When good leaders, good shepherds, good herders guide the sheep, all the sheep contribute and all the sheep prosper together. But some always choose a different path. It's an easier path, a path to power without responsibility. Some always choose to be wolves."

Jeff laid down his cards. His last card was a four, and he hit thirty-one exactly. Maybe, just maybe, Jeff could win this match. Papa knew what Jeff was thinking. He laughed, "Very good Jefferson. But the fat lady has not yet begun singing."

This was a sentiment Jeff knew all too well. He had been ahead many times, even in the final game, only to lose in the end. He wasn't letting his guard down. They each counted out the points in their hands, and Jeff tallied the crib.

Papa took a bite of dark chocolate in his mouth and chased it with a sip of wine. "Have you tried this Belgian chocolate yet, Jefferson? It's a perfect match with this wine."

"I think I will." Jeff followed Papa's lead.

Papa resumed his stream of consciousness. "On an individual level we seek power – control. At a societal level wolves do the same thing. Do you remember the last time we talked about the economy, Jefferson?"

"I sure do, Papa. That was at Thanksgiving."

"Yes. What were those four component parts comprising an economy?"

"As I recall, the four fundamental components of an economy as we discussed" – Jeff made this distinction as he knew economists presented different perspectives – "are physical resources, labor, ideas, and ownership."

"You have a great memory, Jefferson!"

Jeff expounded further. "And 'ownership' is another word for 'control.' Or as we had discussed, Papa, ownership represents the rules of the game."

"That's right. Whoever 'controls'" – Papa made those quotation marks with his hands in the air as he said the word "control" again – "those assets – the resources, the labor, and the ideas – whoever owns the assets rules the game."

And Jeff asserted, "And money is our means to control assets."

"That's right," Papa agreed. "In our society; now; money assumes the preeminent, the dominant, the ultimate position. People dream about it, hope to come into it, and aspire to have it. Because whoever controls the money, controls the assets."

"And that's why Roosevelt confiscated all the gold from Americans in the 1930s," Jeff remembered. "Gold was money. By taking the gold, Roosevelt ensured the government controlled money and thereby controlled society."

"Yes, that's right, Jefferson." Monetary policy was always a popular subject for Papa and Jeff. "At a societal level, for wolves, people are just another resource. Physical resources, labor, and ideas are what wolves seek to control. And money facilitates it all."

Jeff questioned, with a sly smile, "Was it Rothschild or Garfield who stated, 'Whoever controls the money controls the nation'?" Jeff was referring to James Garfield, not the cartoon cat, but this was an inside joke.

Papa chuckled. "What we determine as ownership is what makes control possible. And what that equates to in our modern American, heck our modern world economy, are the rules of the game."

"And for us, this game is played with money," Jeff confirmed, following Papa's stream of consciousness and jockeying to circle back. "So, throughout history, from time

120

immemorial, people asserted, or achieved, or acquired power by asserting **MIGHT**."

Papa emphasized, "Yes. Physical dominance is the predominant theme of human society. **MIGHT MAKES RIGHT**. The wolves howl!"

Jeff went on, "The ends – power and control – always justify the means."

"It seems so," Papa agreed solemnly. "But ultimately, in the end, power corrupts. We, the sheep, want to live good lives. But since most of us don't want to work hard, we rely on leaders. Herders must rise up to lead and show us the way. When the sheep respond to good leadership and pull together, the flock prospers."

"Eventually, though, prosperity sows the seeds of our demise," Jeff added. "Wolves, always seeking the easiest path to power, begin to make headway, and sentiment turns. In time, with the sheep no longer listening, even the herders become discouraged. And the corrosive nature of power takes hold."

Papa added, "Emperors, pharaohs, Caesars, tsars, rajahs, kings, queens, princes and dukes, feudal lords, dictators, despots, tyrants, royals and rulers of all types, even presidents and ministers, preachers and popes: all succumb to the allure of power."

"Servants – the few serving the many – are corrupted by power and ultimately seek to be served," Jeff restated.

"The few always come to believe they are destined to rule the hapless masses," nodded Papa. "By means of fear and manipulation, the servants turn the tables and get the many to serve the few."

Jeff could see clearly what Papa meant.

Papa went on, "The sheep always want benevolent servants – great and self-less herders – to lead them. But that rarely lasts, as wolves emerge."

"Isn't that what the Founding Fathers were striving to establish through the Constitution here in these United States?" Jeff questioned. "Weren't they seeking to overcome our worst human tendencies?"

"By establishing a system of the people, by the people, and for the people," Papa replied, "It was a pretty good try." He chuckled, then continued, "But we, through our nature, tend toward an easier path to power."

"Wolves rise up," Jeff concluded the thought. "And the flock scatters."

Papa's cycle was playing out.

122

"Wolves are dominating the sheep now," Jeff confirmed.

"While the cycle continues," Papa reminded Jeff, "don't think the sheep are powerless. The sheep are never powerless. The power always lies with the sheep."

Jeff echoed, "But the question is, when will the sheep decide to exercise their power?"

"Yes, Jefferson. This is the critical question," Papa said. "We want to be happy. And to be happy we think we must be in control. And in our modern society, we've made money the means to control. We believe money controls everything."

Jeff reminded Papa, "Or at least that is what most of us believe: the quest for money drives our economy. Money dominates our politics. Money is our means to control."

"Most sheep are not willing to step forward to become herders," Papa continued. "Where we are now, the sheep make herding an impossible task. Wolves have risen to power. They dominate and rule everywhere."

"And we, the sheep, are only looking out for ourselves," said Jeff.

"**MIGHT MAKES RIGHT** is how it has mostly been, and is how most societies fail," Papa concluded.

"As power corrupts, herders become wolves," said Jeff.

123

Papa explained, "You see, the powerful begin to believe their own press. They believe they are smarter, wiser, more insightful, and better than the sheep they are supposed to be serving. They believe it's their divine right to rule. They ensure the rules of the game are tilted in their favor. The power is in their hands – they believe – because the sheep choose never to exercise it. Bestowed with ultimate authority and having seized control, the ruler owns everything. Power rests in the ruler's hands. The ruler employs the assets: physical resources, labor, and even the sheep's ideas, all ultimately to benefit the ruler."

"**THE MANY SERVE THE FEW**," Jeff concluded.

"That's not the way the United States of America was meant to be, Jefferson. But the cycle continues: **MIGHT MAKES RIGHT TO GET THE MANY TO SERVE THE FEW**," Papa boomed.

Even Madeleine took notice.

"So you agree with José's assertions, Papa?" Jeff sighed.

"When you survey history, José's dictums appear accurate," Papa replied.

"But what about today?" Jeff implored. "What about here in America now – a supposed free and democratic country?"

124

"It seems the wolves have risen once again," Papa stated quite matter-of-factly. "But do not despair, young Jefferson. The cycle is turning. The power always rests with the people."

"You mean the sheep? I don't have much hope for the sheep," Jeff mused sullenly.

"The sheep always have hope," Papa affirmed confidently. He rocked back and stared into the fire. He then rocked forward and looked Jefferson in the eyes. "On a cold, damp, dark night in Normandy, my Papa assured me the sun would rise. And it did."

Jeff could hear the emotion in Papa's voice and feel the energy emanating from him. Madeleine was alert and listening attentively again.

"The Wexlers and I can attest to that," said Papa. "Father Joseph illustrated the healing power of God this morning when he asserted, 'By the grace of God we find healing.' We must rejoice and find love in whatever trials we are to endure. God will cause righteousness and praise to spring up before all the nations. Christ's healing hand touches us all.

"Pray without ceasing, give thanks in all circumstances. Do not quench the Spirit; test everything and hold fast to what is good. We are called as witnesses to testify to the light, so that all might believe through Him. Make straight the way of the Lord. Rejoice."

Tears rolled down Papa's cheeks. And Jeff's eyes welled up.

Then Papa concluded, "The sheep have never lost the power. The sheep always maintain the power. The choice is ours."

Jeff asked, "How will we choose this time?"

"That, my young Jefferson, is the question."

Papa laid down his last card. Jeff and Papa tallied their points. Papa won the third and final game.

Though he lost the cribbage match, Jeff was taking away something much more powerful and satisfying from this afternoon outing: Hope for **VICTORY OF THE PEOPLE**.

ACKNOWLEDGEMENTS

Everything I have done, everything I do, and everything I am yet to do is made possible by the loving and supportive people that surround me and by those that are drawn into my awareness. It is their genius and their generosity that make my accomplishments possible.

For Lisa, my wife, and my two terrific children, Merideth and Mitchell, and all my family and friends I am forever grateful. I am truly blessed having wonderful people in my life.

To past sages, modern day prophets, and those searching diligently to express truth through insightful words, and lead through faithful example, I extend my most heartfelt thanks. The courage, commitment and sacrifice of men and women who embrace the opportunity that is life inspire me. I pray that the words etched on these pages might inspire you to take on laudable challenges, endure worthwhile hardships, and fulfill what I know to be limitless potential. The world is desperately in need of principled leadership.

ABOUT THE AUTHOR

Scott F. Paradis is a student of life, an adventurer and seeker of ultimate truth. Scott intends to discern, distill and apply simple enduring truths: the wisdom of life. Only once something is made simple can we, do we, truly understand. Striving to simplify the complex, improve performance and fulfill potential, he studies human behavior and compares and contrasts theories and philosophies in disciplines as diverse as economics, business, human relations, communications, politics, philosophy, religion and health and fitness.

Attempting to lead by example Scott encourages people to dream big, build faith and relate to others and life in positive, rewarding ways by establishing life-affirming habits of thinking, feeling and acting.

A native of New Hampshire, Scott completed a 30+ year career with the United States Army. He and his wife, a shining star – the former Lisa Newcombe – currently live in Eagle River, Alaska. Scott and Lisa have two extraordinary adult children: Merideth and Mitchell.

Scott retired from the Army at the rank of colonel. In addition to varied stateside assignments he completed tours in Europe and the Middle East. He served as a National Security Fellow with the John F. Kennedy School of Government at Harvard University and as a Congressional Fellow with the United States Senate. He holds a Master of Science in Administration from Central Michigan University and a Bachelor of Arts in Sociology from the University of New Hampshire.

Scott's personal aspiration is for his life to be a message of hope, an example of faith, and an expression of love as he works to make the most of himself by doing the best he can with what he's got.

ScottFParadis.com
Scott@c-achieve.com
(703) 772-3521

SCOTT F. PARADIS helps people **SUCCEED AT LIFE**.

Through inspiring presentations, engaging workshops, online courses and books focused on success fundamentals, he strives to simplify the seemingly complex and throw open the curtains obscuring simple truths. He is intent on showing people how to have more, do more and become more – how to succeed at life.

Success is not a matter of commanding irresistible power and employing overwhelming resources, it is a matter of doing the best you can with what you've got. You have more assets at your disposal than you know. By relying on your natural abilities and learning and leveraging the fundamental principles of success you can change your body, your mind, your business: your life. Yes you really can!

You have potential you haven't yet begun to tap. Contact Scott now, he can help you and your team succeed at life.

Available from:*Scott F. Paradis*
ScottFParadis.com

SHEEP, HERDERS, WOLVES
Why We Are Where We Are: A Modern American Fable

Explosive Leadership
The Ultimate Leader Training Experience

MONEY
The New Science of Making It

High Performance Health and Fitness Habits
Engage Your Health and Fitness Auto-Pilot

High Performance Habits
Making Success a Habit

How to Succeed at Anything
In 3 Simple Steps

Success 101 How Life Works
Know the Rules, Play to Win

Promise and Potential
A Life of Wisdom, Courage, Strength and Will

Warriors Diplomats Heroes, Why America's Army
Succeeds; Lessons for Business and Life

Look for these online courses offered by Scott F. Paradis:

Explosive Leadership, The Ultimate Leader Training Experience

MONEY, The New Science of Making It

High Performance Health and Fitness Habits, Engage Your Health & Fitness Auto-Pilot

Success 101 How to Succeed, Focus on Fundamentals

Contact Scott now to schedule a presentation, consultation or performance oriented workshop.

https://ScottFParadis.com

Scott@c-achieve.com

(703) 772-3521